Hula Girl

By
gaël P. Mustapha

S0-AEQ-789

ISLAND HERITAGE

Hula Girl

Written by gaël P. Mustapha
Illustrated by Ron Croci
Design by Wayne Shek

Published by
 ISLAND HERITAGE
P U B L I S H I N G
99-880 Iwaena Street
'Aiea, Hawai'i 96701-3202
(800) 468-2800
E-mail: hawaii4u@islandheritage.com

©2000 Island Heritage Publishing
All Rights Reserved. No portion of this book can be reproduced,
modified, copied or transmitted in any form or fashion, without the
prior written permission of Island Heritage Publishing. Printed in
Hong Kong

ISBN NO. 089610-391-9
First Edition, First Printing – 2000

Dedication

In memory of my own *kumu hula*, Aunty Bella Richards
of Kailua, Oʻahu, and the Big Island, and to my husband,
Akema Mustapha, my number one supporter.

Contents

1. Hula / Dance   *7*

2. ʻOhana / Family   *18*

3. Hoʻomaʻamaʻa / Practice   *29*

4. Pilikia / Trouble   *44*

5. ʻAʻohe I Pau Kaō ʻIke I Ka Hālau Hoʻokahi /   *52*
   All Knowledge is Not Taught in One School

6. Hoʻomaʻamaʻa Hōʻike / Dress Rehearsal   *63*

7. Hele I Kahi / Departure   *74*

8. Honolulu / The Big City   *84*

9. Hoʻokūkū / The Contest   *96*

10. Ka Mea Lanakila / The Winner   *107*

Illustrations: *Page 1, 6, 8, 14, 24, 31, 34, 37, 39, 67, 70, 72, 79, 81, 91, 93, 95, 104, 117.*

1. Hula / Dance

Kehau tried to hide her disappointment. She lifted thick, dark hair off her damp neck and then quickly gathered up her *hula* things. She shoved them into the *lau hala* bag Tūtū had made.

Just before *hula* practice ended, Kumu announced the names of the ten dancers who would participate in the annual Queen Lili'uokalani Keiki Hula Competition. Kehau's name had not been called.

Her thoughts raced back to the beginning of the year when Kumu said their *hālau*, or *hula* school, might enter the Honolulu competition. At the time, it hadn't seemed so important. Summer and Honolulu had seemed far away.

Usually, the older senior girls were the ones to compete. They had won local Big Island contests. The older boys had placed in the Merrie

Monarch Hula Festival one year.

The younger, less experienced dancers like Kehau didn't often compete. This contest was special because it was open only to students twelve years old or younger. Kehau wanted to be one of those who participated. She didn't understand why she had not been selected.

She brushed away a tear and pasted a smile on her face. She wouldn't give in to tears here. She glanced at her reflection in the full-length mirror at the back of the studio. The short, damp sundress clung to her lean, straight body. No curves like most of the others in her class already had.

She stood back, watching the other girls wipe their hot, wet faces on towels. Several hurried to the water pitcher, talking in loud, excited voices. Kehau heard Lani tell Malia, "I knew you'd make it."

Kumu touched Kehau's shoulder. She jumped. "Please stay a few minutes after the others go," the *hula* teacher said.

Kehau leaned against the wall. She hoped she wasn't in for one of her teacher's famous scoldings. A perfectionist, Kumu always expected her girls to be ladies and to dance well.

She often said, "No come here if you no like. Others stay out there who like learn," she said in the cut-short, sing-song pidgin English so common in Hawai'i. "They waiting for take your place in this *hula* school if you no like be here." The *hālau* included more than a hundred students, separated in different classes by age and talent.

Kehau knew she danced well. She took her classes very seriously. I love the *kahiko*, the ancient dance, and *'auwana*, the modern ones, too, she thought. *Hula* is part of me, our Pelekane family tradition.

She remembered her grandmother's soft, musical voice the day she started taking *hula* six years ago. Tūtū had said, "It's in your bones, child. Let it come out. *E mālamalama 'oe i kou kālena.* You must treasure your talent. Dance from your heart."

Tūtū Wahine's voice seemed to dance whenever she spoke Hawaiian. Kehau loved the sound of the musical language. *Hula* gave her a chance to learn Hawai'i's traditional dance and a little of the Hawaiian language.

She liked learning about her culture and heritage. It was interesting and good fun to hear the family stories. Reading about Hawai'i's old days fascinated her, too.

Mama and Papa sometimes scolded her for being interested in too many things. "Okay for *hula* and for learn about you family and history," Papa said. "But only when *pau* work. School and home chores come first."

"Let her be," Tūtū said. "The child is born to *hula*, to learn and carry on our family traditions. She is our own *keiki hānau o ka 'āina*, child of the land."

Kehau carried her *lau hala* bag to the front of the studio and set it down near her rubber slippers.

She watched the last two girls go through the gate, their long, dark hair flying behind them in the wind.

"Come," Kumu smiled. "Sit over here."

Kehau walked quickly to the center of the room and sat down cross-legged on the thin straw mat the girls danced on. She looked down. The bottoms of her bare feet were dirty.

Outside the dance studio's large, open window, palm fronds danced in brisk trade winds on the far side of Kumu's big back yard. Bright red anthuriums bobbed waxy, heart-shaped flowers. Bed sheets hanging on the clothesline snapped back and forth.

Kumu's leaf-green *mu'umu'u* billowed about her large body as she joined Kehau on the mat. "I wanted to talk with you," Kumu's dark eyes flashed, commanding Kehau's complete attention. "I want you to represent our *hālau* as the solo dancer in the contest."

Kehau's heart skipped a beat. Her long, graceful hands flew to her face. She let out a squeal. Each *hālau* entered a group. She had forgotten that one girl also competed for the title of Miss Keiki Hula.

She looked at Kumu wide-eyed. "Me? But others…" She felt color rush to her cheeks. "More beautiful, better dancers than me." She stammered, "I-I not good enough."

"The senior girls helped me choose you. You one of our finest young dancers. You now twelve years old. This the last year you have chance for this competition. And," Kumu added softly, "this is my last year for competition, too."

A frown flitted across Kehau's face. It made a furrow between her large brown eyes. "Oh, I want to. It would be a great honor." She must not seem too eager in case Kumu changed her mind. "I have to ask Mama and Papa. It costs lots of money to go Honolulu."

Kumu laughed, patted her shoulder. "Yes, of course. Ask your family. Their support is important. The *hālau* will help too. Remember all the fund-raisers we had." She paused, and then went on, "It will mean sacrifices, you know. You must be willing to work very hard."

Kehau nodded.

Kumu coughed. The sound rattled deep in her chest.

"It is especially important to me this year. My *hālau* has participated in this competition almost every year since it started. I never had a girl win Miss Keiki yet."

Kehau squirmed under Kumu's gaze. "It would be a fine honor for our *hālau*," her teacher said. "This is your last year for chance, and my last year for teach, too." She coughed again.

Kehau wasn't sure what to say. She couldn't imagine Kumu not teaching *hula*; Kehau's mama had learned from her.

Finally, Kehau asked, "Why is this going to be

your last year for teach?"

Kumu said, "There comes a time when others have to take over. I'm tired already. Cough too much. Getting old," she laughed. "No tell anybody yet. Too soon. Okay?"

Kehau nodded.

"Promise me," Kumu took Kehau's hand in hers.

"I promise," Kehau said. "How soon I have to let you know if Mama and Papa say okay?"

"Next practice soon enough. Talk with your family over the weekend. Let me know Monday."

"I will. I will," Kehau said, jumping up. Her dark eyes flashed with excitement as she pushed back a loose strand of Kumu's gray hair and leaned down to kiss her warm, brown cheek. "*Mahalo*. Thank you so much, Kumu." Her teacher's big arms went around her, holding her close for a moment.

Kehau gathered up her large bag, stuck her feet in the blue rubber slippers and hurried out the door. She heard Kumu call, "Plenty hard work, you know."

Out the gate, she skipped down the long, dusty lane next to the road toward her house. Giant, white, ice cream clouds sailed overhead in the bright blue sky. Dogs barked in the distance. She could hardly wait to tell her family and Patty Soares, her best friend.

She so hoped her family could afford to let her go. She wondered if Mama or Tūtū would go with her. She'd never traveled on an airplane alone.

Of course, she wouldn't be alone. Kumu and the other girls were going too. Where would they stay? What if she forgot her dance? Which dance? She'd have to practice hard to make it perfect. All those thoughts and more tumbled in her head as she waved to Mr. Ahuna, who was mowing his lawn. His two little grandsons dashed about between the colorful red and green *ti* plants. Mr. Ahuna shook his fist at them. He yelled, "Watch out for the orchids over there." They paid no attention.

Kehau ran on through the empty schoolyard of Keaukaha Elementary, deserted now in early summer. She noticed the *'ōhi'a* trees she had helped to plant a few years ago during the school's 50th anniversary celebration. The trees had grown big already.

She felt like the luckiest girl in the world. She was proud of her school and the homestead community. Happiness swept through her at being chosen the solo dancer for her *hālau*. She stopped for a minute, hugged her bag close and looked around.

Keaukaha, the small village near the city of Hilo on the Big Island of Hawai'i, was a good place to live, she thought. The community center and the school were surrounded by many homes with big yards. There were no high-rises and only one small store. The beach was just down the road the other way.

The Big Island is famous for volcanoes that

spew lava, which flows tumbling down the mountains toward the sea. Kehau was glad none of the volcanoes were close to Keaukaha. She'd never seen an eruption except on TV. It was scary when Madam Pele, the fire goddess, sent molten lava flying up in fiery curtains. Chicken skin time.

She hurried around the corner into her lane and caught sight of Papa's truck in the yard. She smiled. The best times were Saturday afternoons when Papa was home.

The house stood toward the back of the one-acre lot. Banana, coconut, and *hala* trees grew in a tangled, tropical jungle in the grassy front yard. Hilo's year-round rainfall kept the grass super green.

Mama's spiked bird-of-paradise flowers made bright orange splashes against all the green. Even the house was painted dark green. A large, two-story, square building, the house had an old-fashioned porch all around the front. Kehau's tiny bedroom was upstairs, right under the corrugated, galvanized iron roof. When it rained, the *pak-pak* noise on that roof drove Kehau crazy if she was trying to sleep.

Tūtū's family had been among the first native Hawaiians to move to the homestead. Tūtū had been just about Kehau's age when they moved in.

Mama was born right in the house, not at a hospital. Kehau had never lived anyplace else. She hoped she'd always live in Keaukaha. She didn't want to move to Honolulu like her big sister, Kawahine.

As she ran through the panax hedge separating the front yard from the back, she heard the soft, sweet sounds of guitars and *'ukulele*. She stopped near the first *hala* tree with its deep, upside-down, v-shaped roots. She could see her family, but they couldn't see her.

In the late afternoon, all the chores were done. The whole family gathered in the back yard. Kehau watched them. The scene reminded her of a picture she'd seen in a magazine. She remembered the title under the picture: "Family."

"There is my family, my *'ohana*," she said the word softly in Hawaiian. She wondered aloud, "What will my *'ohana* think about my exciting news?"

2. 'Ohana / Family

The sight of her large family in the back yard warmed Kehau's heart. Papa, her eldest brother Kimo, and her oldest sister's husband, Kane, sat in a circle playing music. Above them, the big royal poinciana tree with bright flame flowers spread like a shady umbrella.

Kehau's married sister, Mele, wife of Kane, sat with her eyes closed. Baby Kalei, not yet two years old, slept in her arms. She rocked him gently back and forth, in time with the music. Tūtū's gray head bent over a Hawaiian quilt frame. Her nimble fingers flew as the needle whipped in and out making tiny stitches. Kehau knew the *hala* quilt design was for Kalei. Tūtū made quilts for everyone in the family. Baby Kalei was special as the first *mo'opuna kuakahi*, Tūtū's first great-grandchild.

Grampa, often called Tūtū Kane, sat on the

ground a little distance away. Near him, Joe, the troublemaking son of one of Papa's workers, helped Grampa mend a fish net. Joe had been living with them for about a month. Grampa patiently taught him to mend the nets used for fishing. Mama sat on a mat weaving a large *lau hala* basket. She worked early every year on Hawaiian crafts for the church's Christmas bazaar.

Only Momi, Kehau's cousin visiting from Honolulu, sat alone and apart, on a rock. She faced away from the group, not doing anything. Her elbows rested on her knees. Her head hung down.

Poor Momi. Kehau knew her cousin must be bored, missing her mother and all the Honolulu excitement she always talked about.

Kehau was the youngest of the five children. Her missing siblings were Kawahine, in Honolulu, and her brother Kaipo, away at a mainland college on scholarship. Someday he would be a doctor. Although the two were away from home, Joe and Momi sort of took their places.

Kehau saw Mama glance at her watch. It was time to prepare dinner. Mama looked up, a broad smile lighting up her sun-leathered face. "Kehau, what you doing peeping at us? *Hele mai*, come join us, silly girl." The short-cut pidgin English tumbled forth easily at home. "I wondered when you was coming."

Kehau ran forward, tossed her bag in a chair. Her towel, the feathered 'uli'uli, and the black *'ili'ili* stones tumbled to the ground.

"*Auwē*! Be careful," Tūtū said, catching hold of her granddaughter's chin and planting a big kiss on her lips.

Kehau kissed her mother and ran into Papa's outstretched arms. He hugged her tight, lifting her off the ground. Kimo tickled her.

"Stop that," she said. "I not one baby."

"Oh-oh," Kimo teased. "I never know unless you tell me."

Mama gave him a withering look; twelve was a hard age. Not a baby any more, but not really grown up either. That in-between time. "Leave her be," Mama said.

Everybody started talking at once. Baby Kalei woke up, stretched his fat little arms, and made gurgling noises. Kehau picked him up and danced him about. He giggled. "Guess what," she said.

"You going bus' if you no tell us what," Grampa said.

"So tell already," Kimo laughed, sitting back down under the tree. Cousin Momi swung around slowly to listen.

"Kumu said I can be in the Miss Keiki Hula Contest in Honolulu. I going be solo dancer."

Everybody cheered. "Good for you," they chorused, each hugging her in turn.

Mama winked at Tūtū. Papa beamed. Kimo plunked a *hula* vamp on his *'ukulele*. Momi asked, "What's the Miss Keiki Hula Contest?"

Kehau explained. Not daring to take a deep breath, she rushed on: "Can we afford it, Papa? Please. Will you help, Mama? Can you go, too?"

"Come help with dinner. We talk about it."

In the big, cluttered kitchen, Kehau got a rubber band, gathered her waist-length black hair into a knot, put on the elastic, washed her hands, and put rice on to cook while Mama mixed the *poi*.

Mama said, "I'm so glad you know, now. Kumu called me last week but told me to keep the secret 'til she told you." She cut up tomatoes and sliced fresh pineapple. "Stir up the stew, honey girl. Papa and I talked about it. You and I will go, and Momi too. Her mama wants her back in Honolulu before school starts." She added, "I'd hoped she'd let her stay with us for a year. She's doing so much better here, but…"

Momi had *pilikia* in her life. She cut school, smoked paka *lōlō*, talked dirty. Her mother had sent her to Hilo for the summer to get away from the big city. "The change has helped," Mama said.

Kehau helped Mama carry supper out to the picnic table. Butterfish, steamed rice, stew, poi, the sliced tomatoes, and fresh fruit. Tūtū Kane said the blessing as the family held hands around the table.

"God bless our *'ohana*. Give us strength and help Kehau with her big responsibility. Help her bring pride on her family and the *hālau*. Let this food nourish our bodies and souls. Amen."

"Dig in," Kimo said. Mama gave him stink eye.

After supper, Momi helped Kehau clear the table and clean up. Back outside, they settled down on the big mat. Papa and the boys played more music. Mama brought out a big flat basket of sweet-scented, yellow plumeria flowers. Their perfume filled the air. As the sun slipped below the horizon the girls separated and strung the blossoms, each making *lei* for morning church service.

Kehau asked, "Mama, you know Kumu's whole secret?"

Mama nodded.

"What Kumu mean when she say this probably be her last competition, too?"

Mama looked at her. "Kumu told you that?"

Kehau nodded. "She stay sick or what?"

Mama said, "She not so young any more. Heart trouble, I think. Her mama died of heart attack."

"But Kumu..."

"No worry. She okay, but I think her doctor tell her for slow down. No say nothing to the other girls. Promise?"

"I promise. I promised Kumu, too."

While they continued stringing the blossoms, Papa lit *lūau* torches and mosquito punks in the yard. Grampa started talking story about how life used to be when he farmed *kalo*, or taro, in Waipiʻo Valley, "Before I met Tūtū..."

Kehau had heard the stories so many times before that she knew most of them by heart. Joe and Momi had not yet heard them all. Momi didn't seem so interested but she kept quiet out of respect for her *pili mua*, her elder.

"In Waipi'o, life hard but good. The taro shaking in the wind. Nothing like it anywhere."

He spun a tale of growing up deep in the heart of an isolated valley on the Big Island's rugged north coast. "Home of Hawai'i's kings," he said. "I stay born there shortly before Hawai'i become a territory of the United States, long before Hawai'i become one state."

He continued, "Lots of Chinese and Japanese just off the boats those days. Those immigrants stay smart, you know. Grow rice and taro alongside us Hawaiians. We was all friends, too. Only way in and out of that valley was mules. No cars those days. TV not even thought of," he laughed. "In fact, we never even have one radio for listen."

He smiled. His old, leathered face reflected memories of far-off days. He pushed his wide-brimmed hat further back on his head. "Steep cliffs, we call those *pali*, go straight up from the sea to the sky." His gnarled, old hand expressed a *hula*-like motion, sweeping from the ground straight up in the air and back down as he continued, "Hi'ilawe waterfall shoots straight down. Icy cold water for swim in. We had good fun those days."

Tūtū laughed. "When he get that faraway look in his old eyes, that mean Waipi'o soon."

The girls wrapped each *lei* in fresh *ti* leaves. Kehau hurried to put them in the refrigerator and

returned to hear Grampa say to Joe, "That's right, Sonny. Soon I take you Waipi'o. Then you see what I mean."

Joe's eyes lit up.

Kehau said, "I like go, too."

"We go then. Maybe next weekend," Grampa grinned.

Later in bed that night, Kehau snuggled under the quilt Tūtū had made for her. Its *'ulu*, or breadfruit, pattern and softness comforted her as she thought about the *hula* contest and all that it meant.

Momi lay on the little cot beside Kehau's bed. "Don't you ever get tired of being here in this dead place, listening to boring old family stories?"

"No. I not sure what you mean, Momi."

Her cousin, who was three years older, sighed. "No more nothing for do here. In Honolulu, we could have snuck out and played pool or met the guys at the corner. Smoke, toke…get some action li' dat."

"Mama wouldn't like me for do that," Kehau said. "Besides, no pool hall near here. Things just stay more quiet, I guess."

"For sure," Momi said. "You such a baby innocent. Don't you ever do things your mama no like?"

"Sometimes," Kehau admitted.

"But not often. This place stay D-E-A-D! Boring!" Momi lapsed into silence.

Soon, Kehau heard her cousin's steady breathing. Momi slept. Outside the window, a million stars lit up the night sky. Kehau thought about the differences between Momi and herself. She tried to like Momi but it wasn't always easy. Honolulu must just make people different, Kehau thought.

Kehau had been to Honolulu, the state capital, only twice. Both times were with Mama. She wrinkled up her nose remembering that even the smells in that city were different. So crowded. People and big buildings everywhere. People could get lost in that concrete jungle. Kehau felt chicken skin rise up on her arms. Honolulu was a scary place.

When they stayed in Auntie Hattie's condominium right near the freeway, traffic was so loud it was hard to sleep at night. No yard. No space. Everybody crowded up. She'd felt caged up in a box.

She knew O'ahu had country, but most everybody lived in the city all jumbled together. She didn't like that kind of living.

Momi's family lived in a poor section of town. Families crowded in small, box-like rooms in a big, tall building with garbage smells in the hallways. Graffiti and nasty words jumped out from the elevator walls. Everything so jam up.

She felt sorry for Momi, having to live like that. Also, Momi's daddy had gone off and left his family. Kehau couldn't imagine her own papa just taking off. Momi seemed hardened by her lifestyle. Tough and rugged. She swore a lot when Mama wasn't around. She made Kehau feel funny kine inside when she went on with her fast talk about what she did with guys. Fifteen wasn't so much older. Kehau couldn't imagine doing the things Momi talked about.

Kehau liked a boy at school. She smiled, thinking about Charlie Titcomb. She had written his name beside hers in the back of her school notebook. She drew hearts around their names.

He's so handsome, Kehau thought, with his green eyes and curly black hair. So tall. She remembered what he'd written in her memory book. She'd read it so many times, she had it memorized.

"To Kehau, the prettiest girl at Keaukaha School and the best *hula* dancer too—fun knowing you. See you next year."

She smiled in the dark thinking about when school started. Maybe this year he'll really know I'm alive, she hoped.

More questions about the *hula* contest popped into her head. How long would they be gone? She thought the contest lasted two days at the Kamehameha Schools, the boarding and day school for native Hawaiians. She needed to talk with Kumu to plan what to wear, what dance to do. So many things to think about, get ready for, and so little time. Less than two months 'til the competition. Kehau hoped Kumu's heart would stay okay, too.

She'd forgotten to phone Patty, but she'd see her at church in the morning. Kehau looked out the window again. *Hōkū lele*, a shooting star, sped across the sky. A sign of good luck, Tūtū had taught her.

She burrowed into her pillow knowing the days ahead would be filled with new experiences. Some strange and different, maybe scary like the big city. She'd have to be grown up enough to handle them, she thought. As soon as she closed her eyes, she fell fast asleep.

3. Hoʻomaʻamaʻa / Practice

On Sunday morning, Kehau woke up early. Hilo's famous misty *Kani-lehua* rain fell lightly outside the window.

After breakfast, the Pelekane *ʻohana* joined the parade of bright *muʻumuʻu* and *aloha* shirts under an assortment of colorful umbrellas. Relatives, neighbors, and friends strolled to Sunday service at their church. Others passed by in cars. Up and down the road, everyone called out greetings. "*Pehea ʻoe?* How you?"

Women looked gorgeous in woven hats or flowers, greenery and feather *lei* headbands. Most of the children wore Sunday shoes that pinched toes used to barefoot freedom. Little boys wore shorts in the sticky, wet warmth of the early summer day. Some hadn't even buttoned their shirts. Young girls wore cool, cotton *muʻumuʻu* or light sundresses.

Kehau ran ahead to share her news with Patty. They stood on the edge of the road in front of the tiny, white, wood-frame church. Patty's long, sandy hair was caught up in a pink ribbon that matched her pretty *mu'umu'u*. "I'm so glad for you, Kehau, but sad for me. You'll be so busy with practice. I won't hardly see you. And I'll miss you while you're in Honolulu."

"It's only two weekend days, silly," Kehau said, shaking her friend's arm and balancing the umbrella over the two of them.

"But you might stay longer, go shop Ala Moana, or visit relatives."

"Maybe. I never even think about that. But it will be so close to school time. You know Mama won't let me miss the first day of school." A frown flitted briefly across her face, then changed to a bright smile. "No make difference. I'll bring you something. What you like?"

"I have to think about that." She tugged at Kehau's arm as the church bell tolled the hour. "Guess what? I got news for you, too."

"Tell me," Kehau said eagerly.

"I saw Charlie yesterday..."

Kehau let out a squeal. "Where?"

"At the fish market. With his dad. He said to tell you 'Hi.'"

"Really?" Kehau rapped Patty's arm. "Not. You making it all up. I don't believe it."

"It's true," Patty said. "Come on. We go inside before you mama give us good scolding."

Inside the church, the sweet fragrance of tropical flowers hung heavy in the air. Flower *lei* decorated the altar and the church railing. So many colors and scents.

Rich sounds of Hawaiian voices swelled in song, praising God, filling the church to overflowing with heavenly sounds. The elders followed the service with Bibles written in Hawaiian.

Babies napped. Flies buzzed. Older children stirred, hanging over the backs of pews, whispering, making noises. Parents slapped fingers busy doing naughty things like poking brothers and sisters or tearing pages of the hymnals. "Shush," mamas whispered in chorus.

Kehau thought about Charlie. Outside, gentle rain rustled thirsty, red *lehua* blossoms.

After the service, families and friends gathered to talk story in the hall, buying goodies from the ladies' bake sale. Children, glad to be free, pulled off shoes. They darted here and there making big noise as they gobbled up tasty mango bread, macadamia nut cookies, and sugary Portuguese doughnuts called *malasadas*.

Kehau whispered to Patty, "I wish Charlie and his family came to our church."

Patty said, "I know. Too bad they don't."

The next few weeks sped by at *hula* practice. Instead of twice a week, the girls practiced four days a week. On Thursday evenings, Kehau stayed late for an extra session on her special solo.

Kumu put all the girls through their paces, reminding them of all the *hula* basics. "The rules important. Discipline." She threw a slipper at one girl who kept forgetting the same step.

She yelled, "Remember, styles of the traditional dance vary from island to island. On our Big Island, home of Pele, goddess of the volcano, the liquid fire of creation lives." Her voice took on a sharper tone. "Pele responsible for this island's growth that going on today," Kumu said.

"Fiery style here. Full of energy. No be lazy. You gotta understand that," she pounded the *ipu*, a large gourd used like a drum, to make her point.

"You must continue to grow in your ability to dance. You look like old ladies with arthritis." Not one girl laughed. They went through the ancient chant again and again.

Kehau's muscles ached. The backs of her legs quivered. "No good," Kumu stopped in the middle of the chant. "*'Uwehe, 'uwehe.* Feet closer together. Lift those knees. Like this," she stood up to show them.

The girls stood like limp rag dolls watching their teacher. She never seemed to tire and never knew when they were ready to drop. A very large woman, but ever so graceful, she could perform every step she taught. "I may be more old than you but I can still out-dance every one of you."

She yelled, "Again! *'Uwehe* fifty times!" Several girls groaned. "None of that!"

The girls counted: "...thirty-nine, forty, forty-one..." Kumu walked between them, straightening a back, holding shoulders still, stepping on toes, scolding, prodding. "Okay, now *huli*, brush, step, *'uwehe.*" And finally, she said, "Okay, break."

Sweat dripped on the mat. Elbows drooped. Pain lines formed at lip corners as girls dropped to the floor, went for towels, and to drink water.

Kumu continued to complain. Kehau noticed beads of perspiration on Kumu's face. She looked tired, but continued to drive the girls and herself.

"Energy. Vitality. The *hula* would never have survived with lazy dancers like you!" Kumu yelled.

Again, she began to tell the history of the *hula*. Sinking into a chair, she said softly, "Long before your grandparents born, the missionaries came to Hawai'i. They decided to ban our dance because they thought it bad." Her voice rose angrily. She warmed to this subject so dear to her heart.

"Fortunately, those who lived in remote villages like ours kept our dance alive, preserved it. Passed it down to their children. The dance tells the story of our culture. Family stories, legends, history...our dances tell of our love of nature, the *'āina*, our land."

She continued, "About a hundred years ago, during King Kalakaua's reign, *hula* gained new respect. *Hula* was allowed in public again. Thanks to King Kalakaua," she gestured toward heaven. "Since then, the popularity of *hula* comes and goes. It's been commercialized, exploited in dumb movies. Some places in Waikiki, they dance a different kine *hula*," she laughed, "for tourists who have a dream of 'paradise' and '*hula-hula*' girls in cellophane skirts. This kine *hula* never part of old Hawai'i tradition."

She wiped a large hand across her brow. "But *hula* survived! In the last ten years or so, it's been revitalized. The importance of the dance is recognized. Okay to appreciate our culture now. The idea of the *hālau* lives again. Hawai'i's dance has survived. You dancers must help, do your part. Carry on the tradition. Teach your own children and your children's children." She sighed. "Some day I be gone, then be your responsibility to carry on. One day one of you will take my place."

The girls straightened their backs, tried to look alert. They didn't dare express a lack of interest even though they had heard this same lecture many times. Grateful for a rest period, they drank water and wiped away sweat. Then they lined up again in formation. Kumu said, "Dance hard so you feel good when *pau*. So you have pride in your heritage, your culture."

Lani stopped. "I so tired, Kumu." At six, she was one of the youngest dancers in the class, and fearless. She'd already been taking *hula* for two years.

"*Pa'a*. Then I make you more tired. I tired, too, but I no quit. No be sassy or act like one baby. Get up. Let's go. We'll run through the chant again. Dance from your heart."

They did. Kumu smiled. "That's better. One more time and *pau* for today." She led them through the chant and then put away the *ipu*.

"Join hands. Let's *pule*." She led them in a brief prayer. Then she told them that Kumu Kamanu would come to watch their next few practices.

"She's more old then me, a very important and respected *kumu hula* here on the Big Island. She taught some of your grandmothers to dance. She can't dance any more. A stroke paralyzed one leg and left her little use of one arm," Kumu said. "But you better dance good for her because she see you mistakes and she scold more worse than me. Just because she no dance no more, don't think you get away with nothing." She waved them away. "See you next time."

The girls hurried out the door and through the gate. Kehau stayed behind to talk with Kumu about her costume and go over a difficult part of her solo.

Kumu reminded her, "This *mele* tells the story of a young, beautiful girl riding through the Big Island countryside. This dance is from the period of King Kalakaua's 50th birthday jubilee, in 1886. You must dance as if you that young maiden. Correct posture and carriage important.

Remember, you will be judged from the moment you make your entrance until you leave the stage."

Kehau danced the song two more times. Then, Kumu said, "Enough for today. But remember to smile. Just because you dignified no mean no smile." Kumu put away her 'ukulele. She clutched her heart for a minute. Kehau knew Kumu hurt with pain.

The teacher shook her head and went on. "Now, I've just about finished designing your gown, a riding habit. In those days ladies wore this kine when riding horse. This competition is a special reminder of monarchy days. Dignity important. Your clothes must reflect that period of history." She took some sketches from a drawer. "I no artist but your *tūtū* say if I make the idea, she find the pattern and sew it for you. What you think?"

It was hard for Kehau to tell from the sketches. Kumu's ideas looked like stick-people. She explained, "This small-kine hat, we tilt forward at a flirty angle. You wear it high on top your hair, drawn up all around softly. With da kine tendrils escaping at the neck."

She moved Kehau to the full-length mirror in the corner. "Like this," she said, sweeping the thick dark hair into a loose knot. "A gauzy veil attached to the back of the hat will hang down your back."

Kehau liked her hair pulled up that way. It was so long and heavy. This way made her look older. Sometimes she wanted to cut it all off.

She studied her reflection. Typical 'ūpepe— a flat, squashed nose— with a sprinkling of dark brown freckles. Kehau wondered about them. She didn't know many other Hawaiians with freckles. Mouth too wide, but straight, white teeth added to her bright smile.

She turned sideways. Flat as a boy. Patty and Malia both wore bras now. "Yuck," she said aloud, wondering if she'd ever grow up. She looked closer, saw a small bump on her cheek. She touched it. It felt like a zit.

"You listening to me?" Kumu said angrily. "I'm trying to explain." Kehau nodded, looked at Kumu.

"The gown will have a small, high-neck collar with white ruching."

"What's that?" Kehau asked.

Kumu explained, "Like small white piping or sort of like a little ruffle. Tūtū will know. And a deep red jacket with sleeves to the elbow and a long, full skirt looped over a ruffled, starched white petticoat. We'll finish off with white gloves. You'll wear high-button shoes just like the ladies did at the turn of the century."

"But Kumu, how I going dance with shoes?"

"You will. They did those days."

"Yuck."

"No yucks." Kumu's eyes flashed, serious, saying she would put up with no nonsense. "You going learn."

"Where I get that kine shoe? How you know all this stuff? Why can't I just wear *mu'umu'u* and bare feet?"

"You like be solo dancer or not?" Kehau shook her head. "I went research this at the library," Kumu said. "Was fun, you know. I think about it a lot, first. Remember what my own *tūtū* teach me from long time ago. Then I get the library lady for help me. Look the pictures, read the books, talk to other *kumu*. We agree. This serious business, you know. We do 'em right or no do at all." She scratched her head. "Besides, gotta do like this for the contest. Too bad I decide so late for enter. I wasn't going to this year. I tired. I not sure you folks be ready. Other *hālau* been practicing months already. So we get hard work for do."

She said, "Now, go take these sketches home to Tūtū. She get the eye for design." She stood back, hands on hips surveying Kehau. "Red right color for you. Big Island color, too. It will bring out your inside glow and the shine in your hair." She paused. "And with *lehua* blossoms, *maile*, and *palapalai haku lei*, it will be good. Just maybe we get a winner if you concentrate, try hard. Remember, this important for me too."

Kehau withered under the close inspection. She felt like she was being examined under a microscope like the bugs she had looked at in science class last year. Kumu seemed to be studying her like a thing rather than a person.

"Scoot now." Kumu added, "Don't forget you going need a garment bag to preserve this gown in."

"I get one," Kehau called over her shoulder, sure she could borrow the one Mele had packed her wedding *holokū* in.

At home, she gave Tūtū the sketches. Tūtū made notes and new lines on the paper while Kehau told Mama everything Kumu said.

They all talked at once, making plans to buy the material, figuring out where to try to get the shoes. The importance of the contest and all the preparation involved loomed large.

Kehau worried, hoping she could live up to all the hopes and dreams — her own, the family's, Kumu's, the *hālau's*. This great honor carried a big responsibility. Kehau got chicken skin.

Again, she thought of Kumu's words, "Do 'em right or no do at all."

4. Pilikia / Trouble

Papa went out to sea again a few days later. Often, his job as tugboat captain took him away for a few days at a time. Joe always acted up more when Papa, Kimo, and Kane weren't home.

After supper, Joe kept teasing Kehau and Momi. He followed them to the kitchen door, leaned against it. His taunts bugged them. He never knew when to quit. "Stupid girls gotta do the dishes. Now wash 'em good or mama going poke you with a stick," he said in a very nasty voice.

Momi said, "Get outta here or I make you do 'em."

"That's girl work. I no have to…"

"Look, you fifteen-year-old creepy *lōlō*, boys can do this kind, too. Nice guys do but then I forget, you not a nice guy," Momi said.

"Shut up!" Joe yelled.

"At least we not loud and stupid like you," snapped Momi. "Can't even live at home you so bad."

Joe yelled, "You should talk. You the one *lōlō*, Miss Honolulu big talk. You the same age as me and you not living at home either. Why you think you here? You no more father even…"

Mama called from the parlor, "Enough, Joe."

Momi stamped her foot. "Nobody wants you at all." She hurled the cup she was drying at him. He grabbed it. He let out an evil laugh and threw it back at her. She ducked but it hit her forehead, fell to the floor, and shattered.

She howled, holding her head. Kehau screamed, "Now look what you did!"

Grampa and Mama arrived in the kitchen at the same time. Grampa grabbed Joe by the ear and shoved him into a chair. Mama went to Momi, took the wet dish cloth from Kehau and wiped away the trickle of blood running down her forehead.

"Sit down over here, where I can get a better look," Mama said, helping Momi to a chair across from Joe. Momi glared at him, biting her tongue to keep from cussing him out good.

"Why you stay? The no good…"

"Quiet," Grampa said loudly. "Why you act like this?"

"He started it," Kehau said. Momi grinned, glad Kehau took her side.

"I don't care who started it," Mama said angrily. "We no act this way in this house."

Grampa added, "For shame on all you."

Kehau bit her tongue to keep from saying, "I no do nothing. Why blame me?"

"You act like savages, maybe we treat you like that." Grampa said, "I talk, act like that when I was your age, my own Papa no think twice. He teach me fast. Hit first, talk later." He sighed. "Why you act like this?"

Joe blurted, "Kimo and Kane, they got their music. Mele got baby. Kehau got her *hula*. You guys got each other. What I got? A big fat nothing." He put his head down on the table. "My mama *make*, die, dead. Ever since she die, Papa no care for nothing. Momi right. Nobody wants me at all."

Kehau sucked in her breath. Momi's eyes grew wide. Mama moved to Joe's side, stroked his back. "We're sorry about your mama, Joe. I know it's hard for you, but..."

"You got it all wrong, Joe," Grampa said. "You got us. We want you or you wouldn't be here. Momi, too." Joe didn't look up. "Besides, I teach you for mend net. You think I teach just any old body?"

Joe mumbled, "But, you old man. Besides, what good is mend net if no go fishing? You say you pay me for help. You don't. You say we go Waipi'o. We don't. You just talk, no do."

"Hey, Joe. I tole you why we no go. Gotta get new tires for the Jeep first. It's a long and steep ride into the valley. Can't go on ball-a-head tires. And Mr. Rodrigues never pay me for the net I make him yet. He say he pay this week for sure. I said I'd pay you some for helping. Tires cost money, boy."

Grampa paused, then went on, "Besides, good for you young folks for learn patience. In this life, we not always get what we want just when we want 'em. Hard fact of life."

Mama added, "But that's no reason to be so mean to Momi. We all family. Treat each other with respect. At least this time she doesn't need stitches, but you could have hurt her bad." She told Kehau to get a Band-Aid.

"You both get *pilikia*, troubles, but so do the rest of us. We gotta learn to get along, even with our troubles," Mama said, putting the tape on Momi's head.

Momi said, "I hope it won't leave a scar."

Grampa touched Joe's shoulder. "I hope not, too," Joe said. "I'm sorry. I just wanted you to…"

"Notice you?" Momi interrupted. "I feel that way sometimes, too. That's why I talk about all the good things in Honolulu so much. It's not all that good, some parts junk. I'm sorry, too, Joe, for what I said." She added, "Kehau's lucky."

"But so are you guys," Kehau said. "Because we love you, too. You part of our family, you know."

She laughed, "Lucky for you Papa, Kimo, and Kane no stay or you might have found out just how much family you are. They probably just like Grampa's papa—hit first, talk later."

Grampa ran his old fingers through his wiry, gray hair and laughed. "I think you right, Kehau, but I'm not sure that's the best way today."

Tūtū came into the kitchen just then. She'd just come from a neighbor's house. "So what all you folks doing out here with the dishes only half done? It's dark already. Should be *pau* by now." She didn't ask why Momi had a Band-Aid on her forehead.

Joe said, "We learning about family."

Momi added, "Old style and new style." She made a face and grinned.

Mama winked at her and smiled.

"Good, good. I like join you folks," said Tūtū. "Kehau, make us all some hot chocolate and get out the Saloon Pilot crackers, the butter, and the good *'ōhelo* berry jam. We finish dishes later." She added, "I think Papa be home tonight. I heard Hawai'i's 'love boat' honking its horn on the way to the harbor." They all laughed at their family joke about the S.S. Independence, the cruise ship that sails between the islands. Papa's tug brought it into the harbor.

When Papa got home later, they were still talking story in the kitchen. "Hi, everybody," he greeted them. "Sit, sit. Don't get up." He walked around the table, kissed Momi, Kehau, Mama, and Tūtū. He ruffled Joe's curly, dark hair and patted Grampa's shoulder. He didn't ask about Momi's Band-Aid, but he did ask her to pour him a cup of hot chocolate. "Two marshmallows, please. I like 'em sweet, like my family."

He told them of his trip. Then, he pulled an envelope from his pocket. "A note from your dad, Joe." Joe took it and asked to be excused. "Your dad said to spend the money inside carefully, " Papa called after him as he ran upstairs to the room he shared with Kimo. "So what did I interrupt?"

Momi said, "Tūtū had just started to tell us about the days when she got in trouble for speaking Hawaiian."

"That's right," Tūtū winked at Papa. "When I was just a small kid and had barely started school, I used to talk Hawaiian at home and at school. We was only suppose to talk English at school. One day the teacher sends me home with a note pinned to the front of my dress. I didn't know how for read yet. That's how little I was.

"We live pretty far from the school. I walk and walk with that note flapping in the wind. When I get home, my mama reads it. It says, 'Lydia must speak English at home and in school in order to learn properly.'" Tūtū slapped her knee, threw her head back and laughed heartily. Her sides jiggled, she laughed so hard.

"I tell you, I never saw my mama so mad. She

tole me in Hawaiian, 'You tell you teacher I the boss at home. You teacher only boss at school.' Of course, I was scared for tell Miss Whitehead, the *haole* teacher, so Mama pin one note on my dress for me to take back that said exactly that."

When Momi was through laughing and had wiped away her happy tears, she said, "So that's why you can still talk Hawaiian, because you kept talking it at home."

"That's right," Tūtū answered. "Sometimes, I sneak and talk Hawaiian at school, too, you know. I know how for talk good English when I need just like you folks, but pidgin so much more easy for all us guys." She went on. "For long time, we no like our kids learn Hawaiian. Like Kehau's mama. She understands but no can talk too much Hawaiian. That's because when I grown up, I only want her to talk English. Funny kine, the way things change. Young people today, they like learn Hawaiian. That's good. I wish I had taught Kehau's mama."

Mama said, "Me, too. But important for learn good English, too. Like Kaipo at medical school. Important for him to know how for speak right. No hurt any of us to know the difference." Tūtū nodded her approval.

Joe came back downstairs to join the family. Kimo, Kane, and Mele came home. Mele put baby Kalei to bed after everybody had hugged and kissed him.

While Momi and Kehau finished up the

dishes, Joe took Grampa aside and handed him a ten-dollar bill. "I want you to have half my money for those Jeep tires. And when you pay me for the net, I give you more." Kehau watched as Grampa hesitated, started to say no, shifted from one foot to the other.

Taking his hands out of his pockets, he said, "Okay, Joe. That's generous of you. It will be a big help. Thanks, and if Mr. Rodrigues pays, we'll go Waipi'o soon for sure." Ruffling Joe's hair, Grampa said, "You a real part of this family for help li' dat." Joe grinned.

Kehau took a deep breath. Relief spread through her. She hated fighting in the family. She smiled at Joe before emptying the dirty dishwater.

5. 'A'ohe I Pau Kaō 'Ike I Ka Hālau Ho'okahi /All Knowledge is Not Taught in One School

Kumu Kamanu came to several practice sessions. She was old, walked with a cane. One arm hung limp in a sling. One side of her face was a little bit crooked. Some of the younger girls seemed afraid of her.

She couldn't sit on the floor so Kumu put a chair in the studio for her. She was so frail you could almost see through her skin. She sat and watched, tapping her cane to the chant rhythm with her good hand. Her bright, dark eyes fastened on each girl's movements. Her good foot moved, tapping the beat. For a long while, she said nothing.

Finally, she spoke, her voice whispery soft in the quiet room. Kehau leaned forward to hear the words. As Kumu Kamanu talked of the *hula*, her eyes danced. Part of the time, she spoke in Hawaiian. She expressed deep feeling through her body language and gestures.

"*'A'ohe i pau ka 'ike i ka hālau ho'okahi.* Remember, all knowledge is not taught in one school," she said. "Your *kumu* teaches you different than I would. That is not to say her way is wrong and mine is right. Only different. She said okay for me to make suggestions." Kumu nodded.

"So why don't we try this?" the elder Kumu explained. The girls tried.

After a few times, their dancing took on a smoother, more fluid motion. The girls smiled and thanked Kumu Kamanu when the session ended.

After she'd gone, Kumu said, "We need to practice in front of real audiences now so you know about stage fright. When we get to Honolulu, there will be bright lights, big crowds. The whole gymnasium will fill up. And TV cameras too."

"Wow!" Lani said. "We going be on TV?"

"Maybe," Kumu replied. "This week, the rest of the *hālau*, the senior girls and young men, will be your audience. Next week, you can ask your friends for come watch. The week after that, we will have a full dress rehearsal. You can tell all you *'ohana*, everybody for come. The week after that is the contest. Barely one month to get ready."

"Kumu, do we need our *lei* for dress rehearsal?"

"Of course not, Lani. Full costumes but no flowers. No forget anything the night of dress rehearsal."

Lani said, "No forget school starting right

after the contest, too. I going first grade this year."

"Good for you, Lani, but let's keep our minds on *hula* until the contest *pau*.

Kehau noticed how tired Kumu seemed. A sadness filled her heart. She wondered if Kumu would be like Kumu Kamanu one day.

A few days later, Kehau and Patty went to Kuhio Mall with their mothers to shop for school things, the gloves, and final touches for Kehau's costume. Momi went too. They bought new underwear, a dress for Kehau to wear the first day of school, and a new *mu'umu'u* for Momi to wear home on the plane.

Patty got a pair of yellow pants with a neat oversized print shirt and belt to go with them. She came out of the dressing room with them on. "Don't you just love them?"

"They look good on you," Kehau said. "Now, let's hurry. We still have to get pens, pencils, notebooks, and paper for school. Mama said we'd all go to the House of Pancakes near Wai&kea Square for lunch as a special treat when we *pau*."

They finished and made one last stop at the drama department on the campus of the University of Hawai'i at Hilo. There, they found a pair of shoes that fit and would complement Kehau's costume. She would have to clean and polish them. "They feel so weird," Kehau said.

At lunch, the girls had big hamburgers,

French fries, and sodas. Patty said, "I can hardly wait for school to start. To see everybody again. Especially Landon Morales," she whispered in Kehau's ear.

Kehau giggled, "I know what you mean. I like see Charlie every day too. Maybe this year..."

Momi said, "I'm glad I'm going home. I wouldn't want to go to a new high school where I didn't know anybody."

"But," Kehau said, "Joe would be going to the same school as you if you stayed. He knows..."

"Oh, Joe." She grimaced, "Joe's a yucky creep."

Mama looked at her. "Not such a nice way to talk about anybody."

"Joe knows some girls," Kehau said. "And when you come watch me dance, I'll introduce you to some of the senior girls."

"Seniors wouldn't hang around with a sophomore."

"They aren't that kine seniors, silly. They older than me but not high school kine seniors. Some sophomores and juniors, too."

"Oh," Momi said. "No make difference anyway since I going home."

"But can make difference," Kehau said. "Maybe you come back again. If you knew more people, made more effort...maybe you'd like Keaukaha better."

"Maybe," Momi said.

"I hope so," Mama added. "You might

decide to come here for college when you *pau* high school. You just never know."

Momi frowned. "I doubt I going college."

"You could if you try, Momi. You smart, you know—only lazy." Mama smiled. "Like so many young people today. Think about it."

Later that afternoon, Tūtū put the finishing touches on Kehau's costume. It fit perfectly. The only thing wrong was that it felt so hot and heavy. The shoes felt hot and heavy to dance in, too.

"I wish I could just wear a *mu'umu'u* and go barefoot," Kehau complained. "Why they wear this kine?"

"The missionaries and Europeans responsible," Mama said.

"What you mean?"

"The missionaries came from New England where it stay cold. They also shocked to find us 'native savages' not wearing real clothes," Mama laughed. "They never realize the real reason why men only wore the *malo* and ladies the *tapa* skirt because was so hot. Our tropical climate. No need for more than that."

"Besides," Tūtū added, "We made our clothes from the pounded *wauke* tree bark. That was our *tapa*. We didn't have da kine cloth to make stuff like them before they came."

Mama continued, "As they 'civilize' us, our kings and queens went *holoholo* to Europe. They impressed with the kings and queens in other lands. Our *ali'i* like their ways so they copy the foreign styles."

Kehau said, "I still don't like it. I think our ways more better for us."

Tūtū smiled, winked at Mama. "But since this *hula* competition celebrates one historical period, you have to dress like that. Besides, it's only for a little while."

"And," Mama added, "You gotta practice in those clothes and the shoes because it will be even hotter under the bright lights." Kehau practiced. She tried not to complain. She remembered Kumu had said there would be sacrifices. This must be one of them.

She also remembered Kumu's other words, "Do 'em right or no do at all." She kept practicing.

A few days later, she found out more about sacrifices. Mr. Rodrigues paid Grampa for the net. Joe gave back his share for helping with the net. "Makes me feel good to work with you. Besides, I have enough money left from my dad." Grampa got the new tires. They prepared for the all-day trip to Waipi'o. They decided to take Momi along.

"Me, too. Me, too," Kehau said.

"You have practice," Mama reminded her.

"But..."

"No buts. You competing for Miss Keiki Hula. Practice comes first."

Kehau bit her lip and fought back tears as she waved good-bye to Grampa, Joe, and Momi.

"Have a good time," she said bravely. "But not too much fun. Ha ha," she laughed. "I only kidding."

She got into the hot costume again and buttoned the dumb shoes. Kehau put the cassette tape on the recorder and began to practice. She just couldn't get it all right. Finally, she stomped her foot and slumped in a chair. "It's too hard. I don't want to do it."

Mama said, "You only feeling sorry for yourself. Why don't you stop for now, run over to Patty's for awhile before you have to go to the studio. Maybe that will make you feel better."

Kehau undressed in a hurry and tore a button off. "'*Auwē!*" Tūtū exclaimed. "Be more careful. No act like one rebellious, impatient child."

"But I not one adult yet. *Hula* is a bore. Too much pressure. No fun. All work. Sometimes, I no like do 'em at all."

"No be sassy," Mama scolded.

"You chose to dance," Tūtū reminded her. "And to be in the contest. Nobody force you into it. No one say it always easy. You dedicated yourself to the dance." In a softer tone, she added, "Some day it will all be worth it."

"If I win, but if I lose…"

"The honor is in trying, Kehau," Mama said patiently. "Can be only one winner, you know. Others have been practicing longer than you. Winning is not everything."

"Yes it is," Kehau protested. "I want to win."

She did not say aloud, "for me and for Kumu."

"Of course you do. We want that for you. But every other girl competing wants to win too."

Tūtū added, "The important thing is to bring honor to your *hālau*. Win or lose."

"I going win," Kehau said, throwing the petticoat on top of the long red skirt and jacket.

"Not if you throw you clothes every which way and make a mess of everything."

"I tired already."

"Of course you tired. In old days, *hula* students stay in seclusion. Away from distractions. Many *kapu*. Make all their implements, costumes. Maybe was better that way," Tūtū said. "*Hula* a way of life."

"I not that dedicated," Kehau said, hanging up the garments. "I want other things in my life too," she said, running out the door.

She hurried to Patty's around the corner and down the next lane.

"When I can come watch you dance?" Patty asked.

"Any time next week, and the dress rehearsal of course."

They sprawled on big towels under a tree in Patty's back yard, drinking lemonade. "Too hot to lie in the sun," Kehau told Patty. "I'm tired of the dance. Same thing over and over."

"If you didn't have practice today, we could go beach. It's so blazing."

Kehau sat up, rubbed the water collecting on the outside of the glass against her forehead. "I know. We might have seen Charlie and Landon there." They giggled. "I could have gone Waipi'o, and you, too. Momi went."

Patty pulled at the grass alongside her towel. "At least it will be over soon."

"Not soon enough." Kehau confided to her friend, "I really want to win for so many reasons, but I'm scared. Wonder if I'm really good enough, compared to the others. Sometimes, the younger, smaller girls so cute all dressed up get more chance." She took the last swallow of her icy drink. "I'll feel awful if I don't win. I feel like maybe my junk attitude—saying I don't really care when I do. Like I didn't practice enough."

"You did. I've hardly seen you all summer."

"I know, but...too bad you don't take *hula* so we could both be going Honolulu."

Patty said, "You know I no like dance."

"I know."

"I'm lazy, clumsy..."

"Not. You just think that," Kehau said, getting up. "We better check the time. I can't be late."

Kehau had almost an hour before practice. They gathered up the towels, shook the dirt and grass off, and dumped them on the washing machine. Upstairs in Patty's room, the girls put on a reggae tape and flopped on the bed.

They talked about how they would get Landon and Charlie to notice them this year. They decided this was the year for sure for guys in their lives.

"At least you got real boobs now," Kehau said. "I don't think I'm ever going to grow. Maybe there's something wrong with me."

Patty laughed. "At least your shirts don't look funny."

"Yes they do! I don't even have my *maʻi* yet," she confided.

"Well, you can be glad of that. Periods are a pain."

Kehau complained, stretching her arms in front of the mirror. "But I want to be a woman," she said dramatically. "And grown up. I'm sick of this in-between junk."

Patty smiled knowingly. "Be patient. It's happening right now and you aren't even aware of it. Besides, the 'flat' look is still in," she laughed.

"Thanks a lot. Some friend you are, Patty Soares. Just for that I'm leaving." She teased, "Remind me not to be there next time you need a shoulder to cry on and a real friend."

After practice, Kehau learned that Grampa had called. They decided to stay over in Waipiʻo for a few days with one of Grampa's cousins. "They so lucky. I wish I was there too," Kehau said.

Mama reminded her, "You lucky, too, girl. You going Honolulu."

"Big deal."

"And you better get hold of that sassy tongue and your attitude. You gotta have good feeling inside to dance right."

Kehau wondered silently if she could ever get a good feeling inside, but she said nothing as she climbed the stairs to bed that night.

6. Hoʻomaʻamaʻa Hōʻike / Dress Rehearsal

By the evening of dress rehearsal, Kehau felt more like herself, not so junk. She felt as excited as before Baby Kalei's one-year-old birthday *luʻau* last year. She had a good feeling inside.

She had seen Charlie playing basketball at school on her way to *hula* that afternoon. He wore blue shorts. She had on blue shorts too. He didn't have a shirt on. Because of paddling canoe and all the sports he played, his shoulders were broad and brown. He had a narrow waist and was so handsome. He didn't wave but he smiled at her when she walked across the schoolyard. He was probably embarrassed to wave in front of the other guys because they'd tease him. It made her happy just to see him. She wished he took hula so she could see him more often. Sports was his thing.

Joe and Momi had talked and talked about

the neat trip to Waipi'o. "We hiked all over the valley, went swimming at the waterfall, and camped out on the beach one night." Joe beamed, "We even pulled taro just like Grampa used to do and we went fishing. I caught the biggest one."

Momi confided to Kehau, "I wasn't even bored. So much to do down there. I helped gather wood, make the fire, cook and everything. Grampa gave us real lessons in being independent, getting back to the *'āina*." Kehau smiled.

Kehau still felt disappointed she hadn't gone but she knew there would be other trips to Waipi'o. She could go another time. Joe seemed more settled, at peace since they came back. Momi, too.

Kehau was tired but excited after a day in the mountains, picking ferns and *ti* leaves for the dress rehearsal. She had helped the girls make their *ti* leaf skirts. Tonight, she looked forward to dancing in front of the audience. When they clapped and yelled, "*Hana hou*, one more time," she got chicken skin. It made her feel good inside even if it had been just friends and other dancers so far.

She felt a special quality about this night. She didn't understand the feeling but it kept growing as all her family got ready, even Joe who thought only sissy boys danced. Boy, he'd be in for a big surprise, Kehau thought. And Momi, too, who thought Hawaiiana was only for *kua'āina*, or "country hicks."

Kehau didn't eat much supper. *Konani* dragonflies fluttered wings inside her *'ōpū*.

Tūtū told her, "That's the stage fright Kumu talked about. Not to worry. It will go away once you begin to dance. You watch and see."

Kehau checked her *lau hala* bag — shoes, towel, stockings, hairbrush, gloves. Everything in order. The garment bag hung on a hook near the front door. Papa said he'd carry it.

Mama swept Kehau's hair up, fastening it with pins. She lightly powdered her nose, and applied a touch of color to her cheeks and lips. "Come on, let's go," she said to the family. "It will take some time to help Kehau dress. Besides, you want to get a place in front so you can see good."

They started up the road to Kumu's house. Lani and Patty met them and walked along beside Kehau, squeezing her hand.

Kumu made a grand night of the rehearsal. She stood in her front yard, her silvery hair caught up in a knot and fastened with a large, yellow hibiscus flower. Splashes of red and yellow, *ali'i* royal colors, danced across her large *mu'umu'u*. She greeted everyone. Kehau thought Kumu looked beautiful, but tired. Teaching so many classes for so many years must be hard.

"The senior girls and young men will dance several numbers first like we all agreed. We'll warm up the audience that way, get them all keyed up for the big numbers," Kumu had said. "And then you come on last, Kehau, as the grand finale." She directed the family to one side of the yard and Kehau and Mama to the other. "I turned the studio and the parlor into dressing rooms for tonight. We going dance outside, under the stars."

Colorful Japanese lanterns and flaming *lu'au* torches lit up the back yard. A crowd already gathered on the lawn under the coconut trees. The warm evening held just a hint of breeze and no rain. The perfume of a million tropical flowers drifted in the air.

Everyone had brought mats, pillows, or beach chairs to sit on. The crowd laughed and talked, waiting for the show to begin.

"Good luck, Kehau. Dance good," friends called as she disappeared into the parlor.

Already, dancers crowded the room. They greeted her as they hurriedly slipped into *ti* leaf skirts, helping one another tie them in place. Kehau didn't need to dress right away since she would be last on the program. She found a space in one corner, hung her garment bag on a hook, and laid out her shoes and stockings. She opened the hat box.

Lani and Malia crowded close. "Ooh, it's beautiful," they chorused. "Let us see your gown." Kehau unzipped the bag and pulled it back to reveal the deep velveteen riding habit. "Ooh," they sighed, touching its softness.

Lani asked breathlessly, "Aren't you scared?"

"It's only family and friends out there tonight."

Malia said, "But to dance in front of everybody all by yourself..."

"That's what we've been practicing for. No time to be scared now," she said. Her brave talk gave them confidence. Inside, her 'ōpū quivered. Momi came in the side door, her eyes shining. Kehau introduced her to several of the girls. Momi whispered in her ear, "There's electricity in the air. It's exciting. I'm glad you asked me to come." She hugged Kehau. "Dance good, cousin."

Kehau said, "I think the senior girls are starting."

"You're right. Let's go watch."

The older girls had begun their first number. Their *ti* leaf skirts, stripped in the old narrow style, rode over white pantaloons, making a rustling sound as they moved. Kehau loved the swish-swish sound of the skirts.

They wore red and white *palaka* cloth tops that they usually wore with long *palaka* skirts for other modern *'auwana* numbers. Barefoot, the girls danced with white plumeria flowers in their long dark hair that shimmered as they moved in the gentle breeze. Stars shone overhead.

The audience clapped loudly when they finished. People stood and yelled, "*Hana hou!* One more time!" The girls looked uncertainly at Kumu. She nodded. The sound of another tune drifted in the air and they danced again. They hurried off the mat and into the studio when they finished. The young men took their places.

They danced two ancient, old-style *kahiko* chants. Highly stylized exercises, they called for precise movements. The dances demonstrated their courage, strength, and agility. Kehau loved watching the muscles ripple under their bronzed, damp skin which glistened in the dancing light.

The young warriors radiated energy. Clothed only in the red *malo*, they carried wooden paddles for the canoe dance and long, finely polished sticks, symbols of ancient weapons. They beat them against other dancers' sticks, simulating a real battle. The sound of the sticks had a high-pitched, hollow *pok-pok* sound that stirred a primitive response, making Kehau think of her Hawaiian heritage with pride.

The audience watched in silence. Only the steady beat of the *pahu*, the chant and the sticks sounded in the air that had grown cooler. Flying feet blurred in a moving force. The *mana*, the power of the dance, filled Kehau's heart. She stood transfixed.

A surge of energy rushed through her. The spirit of *'ohana* long gone, ancestors she'd never known yet somehow knew, swept over her. A feeling of being one with the dancers and the universe felt like a special rainbow around her.

As the young men danced again, she finished dressing in silence. Mama buttoned the gloves.

She, too, kept silent. Kehau walked alone to the edge of the studio. She offered a silent *pule* asking Laka, goddess of the *hula*, for grace, memory, and the ability necessary to present a flawless performance.

When her turn came, she moved forward, poised at the edge of the *hula* mat. She looked first toward the musicians, Kumu and her sister each with a *'ukulele*, and Kumu's husband on guitar. Then, she faced the audience, waiting.

The eerie quiet was broken by the melodious opening guitar chords. Kehau moved through the motions in perfect harmony with the music. She danced in a trance, completely unaware of the audience. All traces of stage fright vanished just as Tūtū had said.

She was only aware of the dance. Her body, feet, and hands told their story. She danced with her heart, giving glory through her performance to the ancient tradition.

When the music finished, she stepped back, extended her right foot, and opened her arms wide in the final position, signaling the end of her story. A warm feeling of joy flooded through her. She knew in her heart she had never before danced so perfectly, so completely in tune with the essence of the *hula*.

For barely a moment, the night was ever so still. Then, the sound of thunderous applause crashed around her. The crowd stood. Still, they

clapped, calling, "*Hana hou! Hana hou! Ka mea lanakila, mea 'oe.* Our winner!"

"Right on!" Joe yelled.

Mama rushed to her side, sweeping her into a tight embrace. "So perfect you danced. Let's hope you do as well in Honolulu."

Her heart sank. She knew dancing well at dress rehearsal was not good enough. Could she repeat the same quality performance in Honolulu in front of bright lights and huge crowds of strangers? She hoped so, for herself, her family, and most of all, for Kumu.

7. Hele I Kahi / Departure

Mama borrowed suitcases. Laughter filled the house as Kehau and her mother decided what to take.

Baby Kalei crawled up on the bed, scooted amid piles of folded underthings and freshly ironed shirts and shorts. He clapped his fat, little hands, happily scattering clothes onto the floor before Mele scooped him up and out of the way. He cried, wanting to get back down to help.

Mama helped Kehau pack and re-pack her bag until everything fit. Finally, they felt satisfied.

On Thursday, the next day, their flight would leave in the afternoon. This schedule allowed time to rest that evening and on Friday before the first night's performances.

They planned to stay with Auntie Pinau, one of Mama's sisters. She lived in Papakolea, another homestead community, not too far from the Kamehameha Schools.

Kehau knew the schedule. She danced Saturday afternoon. In some ways, she wished she was first to go on so she could get it over with. But this way, she'd be able to watch other dancers to compare their skills with her own.

She could hardly wait to board the plane. Momi was excited too. "Be good to see Mom and my sisters and brothers." She said she wouldn't be going to the contest. "We can't all afford to go. Not fair for me to get home one night and go right out the next. I sure hope you win though," she told Kehau. "Besides, I like see all my old friends," she winked.

Kehau worried. She hoped her cousin wouldn't go right back to her old ways and get in trouble again. "I'll pay for your ticket," Mama said. "I'm sure your mom will be happy to have you come with us. Besides, you've been through all the practice and hard work. Don't you want to go?"

Momi nodded.

"It's settled then," Kehau clapped her hands.

Mama made a festive supper that evening. She mixed *poi* and steamed *laulau* that had been in the freezer, then served it outside on the picnic table. Everyone was home. Grampa prayed, asking again for their safe journey and for courage and strength for Kehau.

Papa, Kimo, and Kane played music but

stopped early so Mama, Momi, and Kehau could get a good night's sleep.

Sleep came hard for Kehau. She felt funny kine inside.

Thursday afternoon, Mele drove them to the airport. They squeezed all their bags into the trunk. Mama laughed, "You'd think we going for a year."

Joe, Momi, Patty, and Kehau sat in the back. Kehau held Baby Kalei on her lap. Patty held a plastic bag with three plumeria *lei* inside. The sweet perfume filled the car. Kehau teased, "Why you do that? No need when just going for a short visit."

"I made 'em fresh this morning. I wanted to," Patty said. "It's custom when you go away. To say *'Aloha.'* No matter if it's short or long visit."

Kehau clutched two dozen waxy, red anthuriums she'd picked from the yard for Auntie Pinau. Mele pulled into the loading zone at Hilo airport. Kehau didn't see anyone else from the *hālau*. Most of them planned later flights or were flying over the next morning. All the greenery and flowers would come with them so they would be as fresh as possible.

Joe unloaded the trunk, carried the bags to the counter. Mama thanked him for being so helpful. He hugged Kehau. "Good luck, girl. You good."

Patty put the *lei* on Mama, Momi, and

Kehau, giving them each a kiss and a hug. Everyone hugged and kissed. Mama told Joe, "Help Tūtū Kane while we gone." She squeezed Baby Kalei's fat, little, brown cheeks and kissed the top of his head. Then, they went through the boarding gate.

On the plane, they found a row with three empty seats. Momi sat next to the window. They buckled their seat belts and settled back. Soon, they taxied toward the runway.

Kehau didn't like take-offs or landings. Her stomach churned as the engine sounds changed pitch. She grabbed the arms of the seat and squeezed until her knuckles turned white. The plane gathered speed and lifted off the ground.

Kehau leaned over Momi to look out the window and watch Hilo Bay and the island below grow smaller.

Before long, the plane began to make its descent to Honolulu Airport. "There's the Windward side and Hawai'i Kai, Diamond Head, and Waikiki," Momi said. Big tall buildings all jumbled together amazed Kehau once again.

Traffic below on the freeway looked like tiny go-carts crawling along. Kehau sat back, checked her seat belt, and steeled herself for the landing.

When the plane touched down, she felt a jolt. Her stomach jumped. The brakes grabbed, the motors roared and screamed in her ears. She wondered what would happen if a tire blew out or if the brakes failed. She knew it rarely happened, but for her it was a "daymare" instead of a nightmare until the plane rolled to a stop in front of the terminal. The old ways of going by canoe or ship must have been better, she thought.

These thoughts flew out of her head when the plane stopped. She could see crowds of people near the gate. Inside the plane, they unbuckled their seat belts and gathered their belongings. They moved toward the door with the other passengers and walked down the steps into the bright, late afternoon sunshine.

The airport smelled of jet fuel, flowers, and a crush of bodies. The air not so clean as Hilo, Kehau thought. It stinks.

She caught sight of Auntie Pinau and Momi's mother, Auntie Ella. After hugs and kisses, Auntie Pinau drove Momi and her mother home.

Mama said, "We'll pick you up tomorrow night, Momi."

"I'll be ready," Momi said. "And thanks, Auntie, for the summer. It was good there." She hugged and kissed Mama.

"I know you'll come stay with us again," Kehau said. "See you tomorrow."

Momi laughed. "Who knows, I might come after high school for college." Momi's mother smiled at her daughter.

Kehau waved as they pulled away from the curb. She waved until they had turned the corner.

Auntie Pinau drove through downtown Honolulu. Turning on to King Street, they passed King Kamehameha's statue and 'Iolani Palace, the courthouses, City Hall, and Kawaiaha'o Church. When they neared the street that Kehau knew led to Ala Moana Shopping Center, Auntie turned left toward the small mountain called Punchbowl. The extinct volcano crater today is the site of the National Memorial Cemetery of the Pacific.

Papakolea homestead community climbs up the mountainside next to Punchbowl. Many of the pastel houses along the road overlooking Honolulu are built on high stilts because of the mountain.

Auntie and Mama talked all the way, catching up on family news. Kehau just gazed out the window at everything that was Honolulu, so different from the Big Island. Too much of everything, she thought.

After settling in, Kawahine came over. She and Mama kissed and hugged. Happy tears ran down their cheeks, they were so glad to see each other. "Well, well, little sister," Kawahine said. "You not so little any more. You going win, I hope."

"I going try," she answered. "Why you like live over here? It's so jam-up. Why don't you come *home*?"

"It's called money and job, Honeygirl. You'll find out soon enough when you finish growing up, and *pau* school." She went on, "Honolulu has

more opportunity. You get used to it. This is my home now." She winked at Mama.

"You and Mama have to come to my place while you here. I moved to a nicer apartment since you came last time."

Kehau said, "You must be doing good at your job."

"Yes. I got a raise. I have a roommate, too, who shares expenses with me."

"What kine roommate?" Mama frowned. "You didn't tell me..."

"Oh, Mama. She's a *haole* girl from California. She works in a different section of my office. You'll like her. Nice girl, Nancy."

Mama said, "I don't know if we going have time to come..."

"When you going back?"

"Monday morning," Mama said.

"That's a holiday, remember. I'll be off work. I can pick you up for breakfast at my place. Then, I take you to the airport."

With those plans made, Kawahine said she had to go because she had a night class to attend. "I'm taking a computer course. I want to get ahead in my job."

Mama teased, "And what about marriage and more *mo'opuna* for Papa and me?"

"Later for that, Ma. I'm a modern-day Hawaiian woman. Career first, marriage and babies later. Besides, I'm only nineteen now, you know."

"I was married to your Papa and Kimo was already born when I was your age."

"That's old days, Ma. I hope you paying close attention, Honeygirl," she said to Kehau. "Country is fine. Old ways is fine, too, but there are other ways. No forget that." Kawahine flashed her dark brown eyes at Kehau. "Remember that."

Kehau nodded. "I don't even like guys yet, so no worry." A smile played at the corners of her mouth. She wasn't about to share her feelings for Charlie with Mama or Kawahine.

Kawahine looked at her knowingly and winked.

"You so high muck-a-muck, now," Kehau said. "So *haole*-fied. The way you talk..."

Mama shook her head. "Times do change," she said.

Auntie Pinau smiled. "That's kids today. You never know what going happen. Your Kaipo studying for be one doctor, my Johnny Boy working Alaska, and my Meggie Ann learning plenty kine foreign languages to become...what you call that? Interpreter? Kids different today from when we grew up."

"For sure," Mama said. The strange tone of her voice caused Kehau to stare at her mother. Maybe she didn't like all the changes.

8. Honolulu / The Big City

On Friday, Kehau woke up early. Auntie Pinau's house was on the side of the hill. The front yard was steep and full of tropical plants. Many stone steps led down to the street. The veranda extended the length of the front of the house.

Kehau leaned against the porch railing, watching the sun climb into the day behind Tantalus mountain. A rosy pink tinged the white-gray clouds. The mountains stood like deep blue-green sentinels over the city spread out below. Light still twinkled, giving a fairy tale quality to the view. The slate-gray sea was flat and calm in the distance.

She listened to the wake-up morning sounds. Clatter-chatter of mynah birds in the nearby trees, clanging pots in the kitchen, and the distant wail of a police or ambulance siren. Already, the air felt warm. Overhead flew a *kōlea*, a bird that appears in Hawai'i at the end of summer and migrates to Alaska in the spring.

Kehau ran to the edge of the veranda to watch the *kōlea* disappear off into the mountains. "Oh," she exclaimed, catching sight of a beautiful *ānuenue*, a rainbow. Symbol of the gods, Tūtū had taught her. A good omen.

The day passed quickly. Before she knew it, it was time to leave for the Kamehameha Schools and the opening night of the contest.

Kawahine came to Auntie Pinau's. She brought her roommate. "This is Nancy from California. Tonight we going show her some real Hawaiian culture."

They laughed as Nancy protested, saying that in the two years she'd been in Hawai'i, and before meeting Kawahine, she'd gone to many kinds of local cultural events. "Including the Prince Lot Hula Festival in Moanalua Gardens, and the one they have every year in the country. On the Windward side."

"Okay," Kawahine said, "So you not a total *malihini*. But you not a *kama'āina* either. Besides, this contest more special because my baby sister dancing in it."

Mama added, "And because you going with us. You part of our family now since you stay with Kawahine."

"Thank you," Nancy said. "*Mahalo*. Is that

the right word?" Kehau nodded. Nancy said, "I'm honored to be part of your family." She smiled.

"So, let's get a move on," Kawahine said. "We don't want to be late. Parking may be a problem."

Auntie Pinau and Kawahine argued briefly about which car to take. Finally, they agreed to take Kawahine's smaller one. "No need too much room for park this one," she said as they all piled in.

Nancy sat in front with Kawahine. Kehau squeezed in back between Mama and Auntie Pinau. They picked up Momi. She sat on Auntie Pinau's lap. "Wow, so crowded!" Momi exclaimed.

They drove through the entrance gate to the Kamehameha Schools. The car climbed up the steep hill of Kapalama Heights which twisted in a hairpin turn, leading up to Ali'i Road and on to the gymnasium.

The parking lot was filling up fast. They found a space without too much trouble. "Lucky thing we brought my small car," Kawahine said.

"Tomorrow night we bring mine," Auntie Pinau said. "Momi grew big since last I saw her."

Mama stepped out of the car and stood still. "I always love the view from up here. Look at the sunset," she said. "See, the sun seems to be dropping into the ocean."

They looked out beyond Pearl Harbor toward the west end of the island, called Ka'ena Point. Kehau knew that the island of Ni'ihau, the farthest from the Big Island, lay beyond the horizon across the sea. Only Hawaiians lived on the tiny island of Niʻihau.

The low range of mountains that dipped into the sea looked deep purple against a magenta sky. Pinks and golds splashed in the changing sun shafts that shot up into the sky. The view took Kehau's breath away. From this point, Honolulu looked beautiful. Maybe it wasn't such a scary place after all, Kehau thought.

She turned away first. "Come on, let's go so we can get good seats." They approached the gymnasium. "Should we find out where the dressing rooms are so we'll know for tomorrow?"

"Laters," Kawahine said. "Let's find seats." She led them to the ticket taker, who handed programs to each of them.

Inside the cavernous gym, the seats filled up fast. A loud din rose in the hall as everyone talked at once. Tiers of hard, wooden benches went from floor level almost up to the ceiling on three sides. They greeted friends, family, and several other *hālau* members.

Kehau asked Momi, "Is Kumu here yet?"

"She's over there," Lani pointed to the other side of the gym.

"Are we supposed to sit in a special place?"

"No make difference," Lani answered. We going meet tomorrow morning to practice one more time. Then we all sit together."

"I know about the rehearsal."

Lani said, "Our *hālau* dances at two o'clock tomorrow. You dance after us, I think."

"That's right." Kehau waved. "See you later." She hurried up the steps to catch up with her family. At the mid-level section on the Diamond Head side of the gym, they found seats.

"This looks like a good place," Kawahine said. "Not too low, not too high." Nancy took the seat farthest in, then Kawahine, Momi, Kehau, Mama, and Auntie.

The wooden stage below them stood about two feet off the floor. Behind the stage, banks of large red and green *ti* plants stood in a straight line. Standards of more rolled *ti* leaves interwoven with *maile* and the yellow-orange *ilima* flowers stood in a colorful line in front of the *ti*. These *kahili*, symbols of royalty, were made of feathers in ancient Hawai'i. Smaller green plants in green plastic pots lined the other three sides of the stage to hide the wood and to add a tropical outdoor illusion.

The colorful crowd wore *mu'umu'u* and *aloha* shirts of many prints, reminding Kehau of the *ānuenue* she'd seen. Women wore wide-brimmed hats festooned with feathers and flowers. T-shirts advertised "Suck 'Em Up," "Primo Beer," and "Surf Hawai'i," with appropriate pictures to match. Bright, hot lights made the gym very warm. Across the room, Kehau saw lots of *lau hala* and Japanese fans being waved as the crowd tried to cool off.

The lights dimmed as the program director walked onto the stage. A hush fell as the sound of conch shells filled the gym, formally opening the program.

"*Aloha*," the man greeted the audience.

The crowd responded, "*Aloha*."

The director introduced the *kahu*, who chanted a *pule*. After the long prayer, the director briefly explained the history of the Queen Lili'uokalani Hula Competition, sponsored by the Kalihi-Palama Culture and Arts Society. He told of Queen Lili'uokalani, Hawai'i's last reigning monarch, and her dedication to music and the arts. "This competition is in that grand lady's memory."

He introduced the judges, representatives from a cross-section of the Hawaiian community. He also explained the rules for judging and scoring.

"Posture, entrancse, costume, music, interpretation, exit," and more. His voice droned on. Kehau wished he'd finish. She wanted to see the dancers.

Her heart fluttered. Her hands trembled. She held on to the undersides of her knees to steady them. Momi patted her knee. "Relax, mellow out. Too bad you no like smoke a joint," she whispered. Kehau frowned. "I only kidding," Momi said.

"...And now, let the program begin!" The director announced the name of the first *hālau*. The girls stood on either side of the stage in two straight lines. Kehau sat entranced as they proceeded through the *kahiko* number.

Their costumes looked similar to the ones the senior girls wore for dress rehearsal. These girls wore orange-yellow, high-necked blouses with long sleeves. With *ti* leaf skirts around their waists, and *maile*, *palapalai*, and seed *lei* about their ankles, wrists, necks, and heads, the girls made the rapid, difficult movements. Green and orange blurred against the backdrop of the chant's haunting beat.

The audience roared its approval when they finished. Kehau turned first to Mama and then to Kawahine. "They so good," she screamed over the loud applause, to make herself heard.

The crush of bodies, flower scents, bright lights, and noise created a strange, exciting setting. Kehau didn't feel scared so much as caught up in the electric excitement happening around her.

For the first time, she noticed the TV cameras in the back of the room. They cranked away as the first entry of Miss Keiki Hula came on stage. Kehau guessed the young dancer's age to be about six or seven. She looked just about Lani's size.

She wore a traditional white satin *holokū* with a long train, trimmed with pale blue lace. Her hair was piled high atop her head. A *lei* of tiny, blue, bachelor button flowers crowned her hair. She wore many strands of matching blue *lei* that nearly touched the floor. Kehau held her breath as the girl began to dance.

She moved with grace but the music of the

'auwana was almost too slow. She looked awkward as she missed a step and tried to catch up. Kehau didn't know if anybody else even noticed. Kehau relaxed. She knew she could do better than this little girl.

The knot of fear returned and balled in her stomach as the evening wore on and she watched other contestants. Such fine, well-trained dancers. She felt uncertain, wondered if she could match their skills.

Some of the Miss Keiki competitors danced with their *hālau*. She was glad she only had to concentrate on one number and that there was one more rehearsal tomorrow. She knew it would be too late to practice when she got back to Auntie's. She promised herself she would get up early in the morning to practice alone before joining the *hālau*.

During one group performance, she and Mama went to find the dressing rooms. They were upstairs. One girl was crying. A woman who must have been her mother fussed with her hair and was scolding the young girl.

In another room, she saw girls crowded together, adjusting *ti* leaf skirts, applying lipstick to one another. In an empty room, broken greens, several *ipu* gourds in one corner, and open *'ukulele* cases littered the floor. Empty garment bags and clothes lay in heaps everywhere.

In another area, knots of people—dancers and relatives—posed for photographs. Flash bulbs

exploded in white light.

Back outside, Kehau caught a glimpse of the little girl who had danced the first solo. She looked cuter off-stage than on.

It was nearly midnight when they reached Auntie's house. They had talked on the way about the beauty of the competition. How much they'd enjoyed the program. They stopped at a little place for steaming hot bowls of *saimin* before dropping Momi off.

Momi hugged everyone. "Thank you for taking me. It was exciting and good to be with my family."

Mama hugged her tight. "See, Hawaiian stuff, our heritage pretty interesting." Momi ran inside her tall building.

Finally, everyone kissed Kehau good night. She went to bed.

The bed had not felt strange last night. But tonight, it seemed lumpy, hard, and cold. She missed her own pillow. She wished Papa and her grandmother had seen it all, could be with her when she danced. Finally, she slept.

She dreamed of confused *hula* images, mistakes, loud applause. But the applause was not for her. She heard Tūtū's and Kumu's voices all mixed up together.

9. Hoʻokūkū
/ The Contest

She did not feel very rested when she awoke
early in the morning. As soon as everyone was up,
she put on the tape and practiced and practiced.
Mama told her some time later, "Enough. You'll
wear yourself out and what you don't know now
will not get better."

"But, Mama..." She remembered Kumu's
words, "Do 'em right or no do at all." She wanted
to do 'em right.

"No buts. Rest now. You still have rehearsal."

The rehearsal went well enough, although it
was difficult for the *hālau* to get just the right
spacing. They were so used to dancing at Kumu's,
within the limits of the *hula* mat.

Kumu seemed preoccupied. Twice, she
started playing the wrong music, stopped to wipe
perspiration from her brow with a large rag.

Lani said, "Something wrong, Kumu. How you forget our music?"

"Never mind," Kumu said. She laughed. "I guess I get jitters sometimes just like you folks." The girls laughed.

As rehearsal ended, they all joined hands to *pule*. Kumu led them in prayer. Each girl added a little thought of her own for herself and for the *hālau*. Kehau prayed that Kumu would be okay, and that she could give a flawless performance.

Kumu clapped her hands. "See you all there by one o'clock. No be late."

Kehau had a light lunch; half of a sweet papaya, two Saloon Pilot crackers slathered with butter and jam, and a glass of fruit juice. She tried to rest. Impossible. She tossed and turned on the bed, and finally gave up.

She sat on the veranda and stared out toward the city, going over the *hula* steps in her head. Then Mama called her to get ready.

Kawahine came with Nancy. Auntie Pinau picked up Momi and drove them all back up to the school. Mama carried the garment bag. Kehau carried the hat box and her *lau hala* bag. They found the room assigned to their *hālau*.

General confusion met them as girls dressed, helping one another. Their discarded clothes lay in tangled heaps beside *uliʻuli*, greens, *lei*, and *hula* skirts. Assorted sizes of sandals and rubber slippers added to the disorder.

The confusion heightened Kehau's nervousness. *Konani* dragonfly fluttered wings inside her *'ōpū* again. Stage fright hit her with full force. She thought of Tūtū's words: "It will disappear the moment you begin to dance." She remembered how it happened at dress rehearsal. She hoped it would be the same.

Mama helped her into the hot and heavy costume. The air felt stifling in the room, too small for so many girls. "Hang on to your gloves after you put your shoes on," Mama told her. "You should have put the shoes on first. I'll help you button them. No need to put the gloves on until just before your turn." She added, "We'll go outside where it's cooler as soon as we're finished here."

She brushed Kehau's hair, swept it up, loosened the tendrils and arranged them carefully around her face. "Here, let's put on the *lei* before we do your hat." She separated the heavy *hakū lei* of *maile*, *palapalai*, and delicate *lehua* from the protective green florist tissue in the box.

"Ooh, it's beautiful and smells so good," Kehau said as Mama draped it across her left shoulder and fastened the two ends at her right hip. Mama stepped back.

"You so beautiful," Momi said.

Mama said, "Now for a touch of color." She applied blush and lip color and then set the hat atop her daughter's piled-high hair. She tilted it forward at the right flirty angle and then pinned it in place.

Mama stepped back again with her hands on her hips surveying her youngest child as the other dancers crowded around. Lani said, "You even prettier than at dress rehearsal."

Malia added, "The *lei* is perfect. The green with the delicate red *lehua* and the gorgeous red of your gown. It's rich."

"Pretty as a picture," Kawahine said, coming in just then with her camera. Kumu was right behind her. She sighed and smiled.

Kawahine took lots of pictures of Kehau and Mama, of Kumu with her, and of her and the other *hālau* members. She laughed, "You a vision of loveliness. Like a page right out of a historical fashion magazine," she teased.

"Go dance like a vision of loveliness," Kumu smiled again. "Are you all ready?"

"As ready as we'll ever be," several girls chorused.

Lani said in a small voice, "I scared."

"Just do your best. All of you. That's all I expect," Kumu said, adding, "Let's go down now. Quietly, like ladies. It's almost time."

They followed her downstairs. Kumu's breathing was labored as they waited in the wings for the other *hālau* to finish. Kehau blew kisses to them and whispered, "Let's win." The *hālau* went through the door to perform. Kehau stepped outside into the cooler night air. She held her gloves carefully so they wouldn't wrinkle.

She wished she could go in to watch her *hālau*. But she'd been told to stay behind and wait so none of the audience would see her before her performance.

Another solo dancer would follow the girls. Then another *hālau*, and then the Kehau.

She caught sight of the girl who would dance before her. She must be my age, Kehau thought. She looked especially beautiful, older and more poised than most twelve-year-olds. Her figure was shapely. She's got boobs, Kehau noted enviously. Her dress was fashioned in the style of Princess Ka'iulani, the tragic princess who might have been Queen of Hawai'i if the monarchy had not been overthrown.

Ka'iulani, the unfortunate and beautiful young princess, had spent several years in England. She'd cut a grand path there, beloved by all. Shortly after she returned to Hawai'i, she got sick and died just before her 24th birthday.

The young Hawaiian girl standing just inside the hallway had long, curling, blond-brown hair which fell nearly to her waist in rippling waves. Her floor-length, Ka'iulani-style gown cut from a pale, golden yellow was the color said to have been the princess' favorite. The dress had large sleeves that belled at the shoulder. Its high neck framed her lovely, golden face. The bodice, made entirely of delicate, yellow lace ruffles showed off her shapely

— almost womanly — figure. The long skirt billowed gracefully over a hoop. She, too, wore shoes and long white gloves. A wide-brimmed hat and a *lei* of baby yellow rosebuds and maidenhair fern completed the golden picture.

She's so beautiful, Kehau thought. As beautiful as last night's sunset, but more like a golden sunrise. She fought against her feeling of envy. She smiled at the young girl, who returned a shy smile before taking her place near the entrance door.

Kehau heard the thunder of applause as her own *hālau* burst through the door separating the gym from the hallway and the stairs leading to the dressing rooms. She moved closer, calling, "How was it? You did good?" Their broad, beaming smiles gave her the answer. They ran upstairs to change, hoping to get back into the audience in time to watch Kehau.

Mama helped with the gloves, buttoning each of the tiny buttons in place. They moved closer to the entrance but stayed out of the way of the *hālau* lining up to dance ahead of her. The Ka'iulani dancer floated out through the door and past them wearing the same kind of smile the girls in Kehau's *hālau* had worn.

The yellow skirt disappeared down the hall. Kehau turned back toward the door, waiting for the *hālau* ahead of her to finish.

After what seemed like forever, they came

it. When the last girl passed, Kehau moved through the door. Her eyes grew wide. The bright lights blinded her. The size of the crowd stunned her from this angle. She felt *konani* dragonfly wings beat faster.

Slowly, gracefully, she moved toward the two steps leading up onto the stage. She hoped she wouldn't trip or fall. That would mean points lost for sure.

Kehau moved onto the stage. She felt her dress catch. For two seconds, she hesitated, not knowing if she should move back or forward to unloose it. She told herself, "Be calm, don't panic."

She took hold of a fold of her dress near her left hip and lifted with a gentle but firm swish. The dress moved free of whatever it had caught on. She breathed deeply, looked to the right and nodded to the musicians. Kumu smiled at her.

Kehau posed, standing straight with her right hand extended gracefully above her head. Her left arm made a slow, sweeping motion to encompass the audience as she waited for the music to begin.

She hoped her trembling knees were not causing her gown to flutter. She smiled on the outside, wishing away the *konani* dragonfly wings inside.

The music sounded. The vamp was wrong. It caught her off guard. What was Kumu doing? Instead of starting to dance, she held her pose, wondering how to signal Kumu.

She couldn't figure out what was happening. Panic and confusion gripped her. She swayed, feeling faint. "Don't," she whispered, trying not to frown. She didn't want to embarrass everyone— herself, Kumu, family, friends. The room whirled and blurred as the wrong introduction continued. She continued to hold her pose. She sensed the audience holding its breath. She held hers, too. Silently, she pleaded, oh please, let Kumu realize her mistake.

Kumu seemed to sway as Kehau's vision blurred and then, after what seemed like an hour but was in fact only a few seconds, the musicians started the right music. Kehau began to dance, floating across the stage from one side to the other. She was aware that her dance flowed smoothly. She went through the motions almost like a robot. She knew the steps but something was missing. She wasn't sure what it was.

Still aware of the audience and the almost disastrous beginning, she could not recapture the perfection of the dress rehearsal. The last verse began.

"*Ha'ina ia mai...*" The words that meant "This is the end of my story."

Finishing the last verse, she dropped into a deep, graceful curtsey. She paused, rose, and as the final refrain of her exit music sounded, she moved toward the step on the opposite side of the stage. As the music finished, she stood with her right foot pointed, raised her right arm in a motion similar to

the initial pose. She beamed a radiant smile around the gym, brought her fingers to her lips and blew kisses to the audience.

They clapped loud, rose to their feet. They continued to clap as she backed down the step carefully, turned, and walked with grace toward the door. Once behind the door, she let out a big sigh. It was done. A few members of the next *hālau*, waiting to make their entrance, giggled. "Did you do good?" She smiled and walked on past them.

Kehau knew she'd done well, but not as well as at the dress rehearsal. The wrong music had thrown her off, but there was more to it than that.

She stood alone on the steps outside, cooling off. Perspiration trickled down her arms. Disappointment welled within her. She had wanted a perfect, flawless performance. She worried about Kumu, too.

At that moment, Mama, Auntie, Momi, Kawahine, and Nancy came around the corner, engulfing her in their embraces. She slumped against Mama. "I don't think I won," she said before any of them could say a word. "I danced better at dress rehearsal." She added quietly, "The wrong music..."

"I know," Mama patted her shoulder. "It's too early to tell."

"Honeygirl, you were..." Kawahine groped for the right words. "...movingly beautiful." Tears streamed down Kawahine's cheeks. "My own little ster and what a bummer about the music. You were mature beyond your years to hold the pose and not start to cry or something."

"I'm impressed," Auntie added. "You carry on the Pelekane family tradition in a fine manner."

Nancy said, "It was kind of funny watching Kumu. It was like in the Sunday comics. When she realized she was playing the wrong music, you know, with the light bulb above her head that finally came on. Under all the circumstances, you were the best," Nancy said, hugging Kehau close.

Momi added, "I'm so glad you made me come. It was special to be with our 'ohana."

Mama hugged Kehau again but said nothing.

Later, in the dressing room, the girls from the hālau all congratulated and heaped praise on her. Kehau eagerly pulled off the high-buttoned shoes and the hot gown. She changed to shorts and a T-shirt. After they moved away from the crowd and when Mama and Kehau were finally alone, her mother said, "You right, Kehau. You didn't dance with the magic of the dress rehearsal. But no matter, you danced beautifully. Win or lose, you my winner. You bring honor to our family and to your hālau. You must remember that."

Kehau hid her face against her mother's pale green mu'umu'u. Silent tears spilled down her cheeks. "Mama, Kumu..."

"I know, Honeygirl. Just pray that she'll be all right."

10. Ka Mea Lanakila / The Winner

The final evening, after a hurried fast food supper, they rushed back to the gym. Kehau got back into the hot, heavy costume to await the judges' decisions. Throughout the festival, she had watched most of the solo performers with interest. None of them were as beautifully costumed as the girl in the yellow Princess Ka'iulani-style gown. Kehau had not seen her dance, so she had no idea if her style and performance matched the exquisite costume. If so, that girl just might be Miss Keiki Hula, Kehau thought.

She picked up a program off the dressing-room floor. She read down the list. The girl's name was Victoria Ka'iulani Vincent. A perfect name, Kehau thought. Princess Ka'iulani's English name had been Victoria. She read over the names again. One girl, Jana, who danced Friday night, had been really good, too.

It must be hard to choose the very best dancer. Kehau was glad she did not have to judge and pick the winners.

So many of the *hālau* had been so very good. Grace, style, continuity, arms at exactly the right height; everything came together in a performance. She wished she'd been able to watch her own *hālau*. She knew how good they were. It was hard to know how they compared with other groups when they performed.

She went downstairs. Dancers, family members, and others milled around in a state of suspense. Whispered conversations hummed in the hall. Reports filtered back. "Any time now. They just about ready to announce the awards."

"The judges get hard time," someone said.

"Hush, too much noise back here. They ready for start."

A quiet filled the hall as the director moved to the microphone. "Ladies and gentlemen, and *keiki* too," he began. "It has not been easy. I want you to know that in some cases, only one or two points separate our winners. Truly, they are all winners and should be proud of their participation and contribution to the perpetuation of the *hula*."

He continued, "The pressure is tremendous; the competition keen. I'm sure you are all as anxious as I am to know who the winners are." He added, "I think I can honestly say I am glad I'm not a dancer or a judge." The audience laughed.

Lani jumped up and down. "Oh, hurry, please. I can't stand not knowing for another minute and I gotta go *lua*." *Hālau* members giggled.

"Go, hurry up. We tell you who won if they announce before you get back," Malia said. Lani ran down the hall into the bathroom.

The director thanked all those who had helped with the contest. He introduced the judges again, and some other dignitaries. He talked about the prizes. "Cash awards in two divisions of *kahiko* and *'auwana*. We wish everyone could win." He went on, "Trophies for the winning *hālau* and the solo dancer runners-up. They will also receive commemorative medallions. Miss Keiki Hula's will be of solid gold, contributed by one of Hawai'i's favorite sons, famous in the entertainment business, Danny Kaleikini."

Finally, the director said, "And now, without further ado, the winners." He explained that *hālau* winners would be announced first. "Then, Miss Keiki Hula."

He called the names of two *hālau*. The crowd roared as they went to the stage to receive their awards.

Each time, Kumu's *hālau* members caught their breath and let it out. Sighs of disappointment escaped from them. Tears trickled down Lani's cheeks. "It would have been such an honor to win since I only six years old."

"Don't cry," Kehau patted her shoulder. "It's okay. That was only the runner-up honors. We still get chance."

The director said, "And the overall *kahiko* division winner is..." Pandemonium broke out as Kumu's *hālau* jumped up and down and pounded each other on the back. They hugged, kissed, cried. "We did it! We did it! First place."

Kehau told Lani, "Cry now, cry for happy."

Kumu said, "On stage now. With dignity, ladies."

After they received their awards, came off the stage, and were back in the hall, the sound of the applause still thundered. Kumu said, "Well done, girls. I'm pleased and proud. I knew you could do it." Tears streamed down her face. She coughed and clutched her heart. The girls continued to hug and kiss and cry together.

"Quiet now," Kumu commanded. "They're starting to announce the winners for Miss Keiki Hula. Come, Kehau, up here."

Kehau moved in front of Kumu, who placed her hands on Kehau's shoulders. She squeezed lightly, whispering in Kehau's ear, "I'm so sorry about the music mix-up. Your composure was excellent. Relax. We talk more about it later."

Kehau said, "Are you feeling okay?"

"We talk more about it later," Kumu put a finger to her lips. "Shush, just listen to what the announcer say."

Kehau's heart beat hard in her chest, sounding loud in her ears. She sucked in her breath, afraid to move.

She hoped. She said a silent prayer, "Let it be me." She felt heat rise in her cheeks as she realized that was not a good way to pray.

She felt a strong urge to run. Out the door, down the hill, away from the Kamehameha Schools to find a safe place to hide. But then she'd never know who won. And she knew she couldn't hide forever, nor could she do that to Kumu or her family.

She stood mute. The director's voice droned on. "Each of these girls is deserving, a fine dancer. The points are so close. I will announce the names of the winners in this order — third, second, and first runners-up, and then, last, this year's Miss Keiki Hula."

Kehau thought of beauty pageants she'd seen on TV. How the girls often wept when their names were called. She'd seen disappointment register on the faces of the girls who didn't win.

The audience hushed as the voice over the microphone announced, "Third runner-up is Jana Leialoha DeSilva of ...." He pronounced the long Hawaiian name of her O'ahu *hālau*.

Kehau said, "She is the one who danced Friday night. I knew she was good." The young girl proceeded to the stage in the same orange costume that was not quite floor length. Kehau estimated her age at about eight.

Kehau's hands began to perspire inside her gloves as the director announced the second runner-up. The little girl in the traditional white satin *holoku* with the blue lace trim who had been the first solo dancer on Friday.

Kehau's heart sank. Two very young girls so far. Only one more runner-up and then Miss Keiki. She bit her lip, tried to hold back the tears that welled up. She wasn't out yet. She still had a chance. She'd wanted so much to win. Her last year to compete, next year she'd be thirteen—too old.

For her, it wasn't enough that the *hālau* had won first place. She was glad for them but she hadn't danced with them. She'd danced alone. She wanted to carry home her own share of the honor and glory.

She felt Kumu's hand tighten sharply on her shoulder and then push her forward. She'd been so lost in her own thoughts she hadn't heard the name of the first runner-up.

The director repeated, "First runner-up, Miss Kehaulani K. Pelekane, twelve years old." He continued with the name of her *hālau* and said, "She is from Keaukaha homestead on the Big Island of Hawai'i."

Kehau moved toward the stage as if floating in a slow-motion dream. The director said, "I might tell you our very first Miss Keiki Hula was also a Keaukaha homestead girl. And Kehaulani represents the *hālau* that took first *kahiko* honors here tonight."

Kehau stepped onto the stage. The audience cheered as she accepted the trophy, a bouquet of long-stemmed red roses, and an envelope. She could hardly hold everything. The well-known island entertainer Mr. Kaleikini, who had grown up in Papakolea, tried to place the medallion around her neck. The chain wasn't long enough to go over her hat, so he draped it over her arm. He kissed her, whispering his congratulations.

She smiled, curtsied, and took her place next to the other two runners-up. Tears streamed down her cheeks. She couldn't believe she was crying. Just like those girls on TV. She wasn't sure if she was crying for sad or happy. She was happy to win first runner-up, but she had wanted to be Miss Keiki Hula, who was now walking to the stage in her beautiful yellow Princess Kaʻiulani-style gown.

She carried herself regally. Just like a real princess, Kehau thought. "Victoria Kaʻiulani Vincent, Miss Keiki Hula!" White light exploded. The noise of the audience was a deafening roar.

Later, in the dressing room, the picture-taking and congratulations finally slowed down. Kehau changed clothes. Her tears continued to fall. She blurted out to Mama, "It was too hard. Too much pressure. Wrong music and everything. I don't think I can ever dance again." She hurried

... forgot to ask Laka, the *hula* goddess, for with a flawless performance. My mistake and ...mu's wrong music. It's too much. No more."

Mama scolded her. "Shame on you. You came away with good honors. How many times you prayed. You talk silly because you tired. You complain for nothing." She removed the hat, placed it back in the special box. "You'll feel different in the morning."

Kehau frowned. Mama didn't understand. As they left the dressing room, Kehau caught sight of Victoria. She ran to her and said, "Congratulations. You one very special Miss Keiki Hula."

Vicky hugged her and said softly, "*Mahalo.*"

Momi told her cousin, "You know, Kehau, I think I going take *hula* too. A good way for stay out of trouble, I think. Keeps you busy." She added, "We get one *hālau* at the center. I going sign up." Kehau grinned.

Kumu came up to Kehau. She embraced her tightly. "You brought honor to all of us. You made me so happy. Sorry about the music. Winning is not everything. We both did our best." Kumu slumped heavily into a nearby chair. "Whew, I tired," she said, mopping perspiration from her brow with a towel.

On the plane going home, she told Mama, "I'm sorry about what I said yesterday. And, glad I didn't tell everybody, especially Kumu. That would have been shame and ungrateful."

Mama told her that Kumu had been take
to the hospital in the middle of the night.
"Suffering from exhaustion. Her heart just not s
strong any more."

Tears rolled down Kehau's cheeks. "I hope
she will be okay, that she can still teach again."

Mama hoped so, too. "We'll know more in a
few days."

Kehau said, "I will dance again. I will carry
on the tradition of the *hula*. Maybe one day, I be
kumu and teach one good dancer who will be Miss
Keiki for Kumu's honor."

Mama smiled and patted her arm. "Your and
our *'ohana* can be proud of you."

Kehau settled back in her seat and looked out
the window as Hilo Bay came into view. She
hugged Patty's present to her and whispered a little
prayer for Kumu. At home, maybe they would all
get to see the festival on TV next month. Maybe
even Charlie would see it.

"It's good to be going home," Kehau said to
her mother.

Mama leaned over and kissed the top of her
head. "You truly a homestead girl, our *hula* girl."

Kehau smiled.

PAU

About the Author

gaël Mustapha lived in Hawai'i for 30 years. She studied *hula* for ten years and learned about homesteading in Hawai'i when she worked for the Department of Hawaiian Homelands. She currently lives in Green Valley, Arizona, with her husband. Writing and traveling are her passions.

...ossary

ʌina. Land, earth.

Aliʻi. Chief, king, queen, royal.

Ānuenue. Rainbow.

ʻAuwana. Modern hula.

Auwē. Alas, oh dear.

Haku. To weave, as a lei.

Hālau. Long house or school for hula instruction.

Hana hou. To do again, repeat, encore.

Haole. White person; formerly, a foreigner.

Hele mai. Come in.

Hōkū lele. Shooting star.

Holoholo. To go for a walk, ride, sail, or all around.

Holoku. A loose, seamed dress with a train.

Hoʻomaʻama. Practice.

Hoʻokūkū. Competion

Hula. Hawaiʻi's native dance.

Huli. To turn.

ʻIliʻili. Pebbles or smooth stones used in dances.

ʻIlima. Shrub bearing yellow flowers used in lei-making.

Ipu. The bottle gourd used in hula dances.

Kahiko. Old, ancient style of dance.

Kāhili. Feather standard symbolic of royalty.

Kahu. Honored attendant, pastor.

Kama'āina. Native-born.

Kani-lehua. Mist-like rain famous on the Big Island.

Kapu. Taboo, prohibited, forbidden.

Keiki. Child.

Kōlea. Pacific golden plover, a migratory bird that comes to Hawai'i in late summer.

Konani. Name for a dragonfly.

Kua'āina. Country person.

Kumu. Teacher

Kumu hula. Hula teacher

Kupuna. Ancestor, grandparent.

Laka. Hula Goddess.

Lau hala. Pandanus leaf, used for weaving.

Lau lau. Package of ti leaves containing fish or meat.

Lehua. Flower of the 'ōhia tree.

Lei. Garland of flowers, leaves, shells, or other materials.

Lōlō. Numb, stupid.

Toilet.

ʻau. Hawaiian feast.

Mahalo. Thank you.

Mai. Menstruation.

Maile. A native twining shrub with fragrant leaves used for lei-making.

Make. Dead.

Mālamalama. To enlighten, treasure.

Malihini. Newcomer.

Malo. Loincloth worn by males.

Mana. Supernatural, divine power.

Mele. Song, chant.

Moʻopuna. Grandchild.

Muʻumuʻu. A loose fitting dress.

ʻOe. You.

ʻOhana. Family.

ʻŌhelo. A small shrub with a red or yellow berry used for jams and jellies.

ʻŌhia. A type of tree.

Ōpū. Stomach.

Pahu. Drum.

Paka lōlō. Marijuana.

Palaka. Block-print cloth.

Palapalai. A native fern.

Pali. Cliff, steep hill.

Pau. Finished, the end.

Pilikia. Trouble.

Poi. Traditional Hawaiian dish made from pounded taro root.

Tapa (Kapa). Cloth made from the wauke or māmaki tree bark.

Tūtū (Kūkū). Grandmother (in this story). Otherwise, refers to any elder relative or close family friend.

Ti (Ki). A broad-leafed plant; leaves used for making hula skirts.

'Uli'uli. A gourd rattle.

'Ulu. The breadfruit tree, or its fruit.

'Ūpepe. Flat-nosed.

Uwehe. Hula step.

Wahine. Woman, female.

Wauke. Paper mulberry tree whose bark was made into tapa.

...pau ka ʻike i ka hālau hoʻokahi.	All knowledge is not taught in one sch
...malama ʻoe i kou kālena.	Treasure your hula.
...e i kahi.	Departure.
...loʻomaʻamaʻa Hōʻike	Dress Rehearsal
Ka mea lanakila.	The winner.
Pehea oe?	How are you?

Other chapter book favorites from
The Adventures in Hawaii Series

Makoa and The Place of Refuge

Written by Jerry Cunnyngham
Illustrated by Sharon Alshams

Makoa is running for his life!... This tale of old Hawaii is about a young boy, Makoa, who has broken a great *kapu* which condemns him to death. Can he reach *Pu'uhonua o Honaunau* (the Place of Refuge) before his pursuers put a spear through his heart?

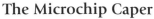

The Microchip Caper

Written by Robert Graham
Illustrated by Sharon Alshams

Julie and Todd have sailed with their parents and their pet parrot from California to Hawaii. In Honolulu, they became friends with Moana and Kai. The new friends are soon creeping onto a strange boat in the middle of the night as they try to solve the mystery of *The Microchip Caper.*

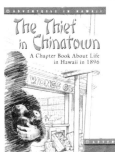

The Thief in Chinatown

Written by Elaine Masters
Illustrated by Sharon Alshams

There is big trouble in Honolulu's Chinatown in 1896! Six oranges have been stolen from Wong's Grocery. The thief turns out to be a runaway boy from a ship in the harbor. Excitement builds as the Wong family tries to hide and protect the boy who stole their oranges.

Surfer Boy

Written by gaël Mustapha
Illustrated by Ron Croci

Surfer Boy chronicles the contemporary story of a 15-year old boy who lives in Laie on the island of Oahu. The story focus is on surfing, getting a driver's license, first love, family relationships, and friendships.